To Climb a Mountain

He knew the way was up
but was he prepared for the climb?

Peter Thomas

RIVER BIRCH PRESS

Daphne, Alabama

River Birch Press
P.O. Box 868
Daphne, AL 36526

Table of Contents

1   He'll Never Make It!   *1*
2   To Love or Not To Love   *5*
3   To Be or To Climb?   *8*
4   Shaking the Foundations   *11*
5   "Run Aways" and "Climb Alones"   *14*
6   Circular Routes and Wisdom   *19*
7   Pay Careful Attention   *24*
8   Daddy! Come Home!   *27*
9   Clean Hands and Pure Hearts   *29*
10   The Valley of Despair   *33*
11   Planting Much for Little Return   *39*
12   The Mother of All Lies!   *43*
13   Faith, Hope, Love, and Comparison   *47*
14   A Twist in the Tail   *53*
15   Shortcut to the Summit   *54*
16   Further Encounters with Fear   *59*
17   Fast Growth   *63*
18   Who's in Control?   *67*
19   Valley Fears, Mountain Views   *70*
20   The Overhang   *73*
21   The Toughest of Choices   *78*
22   Father, Can I Forgive?   *80*
23   Grace and Beauty   *84*
24   Equipped To Climb   *87*
25   The Shade of a Juniper Tree   *89*
26   The Clearing   *92*
27   Pride Comes Before a Fall   *96*
28   Weapons for War   *100*
29   Tears of Joy   *104*
30   Who Am I?   *106*
31   The Summit   *108*
Afterword   *109*

*See, I am sending an angel ahead of you
to guard you along the way and to bring you
to the place I have prepared.*

—Exodus 23:20

1

He'll Never Make It!

"Call Luke to the summit, Gabriel."

"All right. I'll go and tell him right away. Only one thing, God, haven't you called him to the summit enough? It's just that I always seem to be giving him the same message: 'Luke, the Father is calling you. Go to the summit. He's waiting for you.'"

"Gabriel, call Luke to the summit for my sake."

"Yes, I'm going right away. But God, why do you keep calling Luke to the summit? It's not like you don't have enough people to see on the mountain. There's a whole stream of people, even some little children, and some who, forgive me, Father, but there are some who, well, I don't know how even you could use them. So why do you insist on calling someone as slow as Luke?"

"Gabriel, are you still there?"

"Yes, God, I'm still here."

"Gabriel? Do you still believe I am the same yesterday, today, and forever?"

"Yes, of course I do! What kind of question is that?"

"Did you call Luke to the summit already?"

"Uh, no, I am on my way, but I have a question about that."

"I know, Gabriel, but while you keep asking me questions about 'that,' Luke keeps waiting to hear my invitation to come up the mountain."

"But that's just it, God. Why is it so important that I ask him again? He has kept you waiting on the mountain for years.

Why can't I keep him waiting just a little while?" [Hebrews 13:8, Zechariah 1:13]

"Gabriel, dear Gabriel. How I love you, Gabriel!"

"I know, Abba, but please don't change the subject. This is important, and I think we deserve an answer!"

"We? Who is this we?"

"All of us. Michael, me, all the angels. We watch you time and again send messages to Luke. Some of them are so clear and obvious. Yet he starts out and then finds some reason to stop, go back, and sometimes even pretends he didn't hear you."

"Michael too? Haaaa! You two make me laugh. Let me ask you a question. Why are you so concerned about Luke? Why do you keep asking questions about him?"

"Well, Abba, it seems that every time you send us to Luke, there is like, well, it looks like anyway . . . Oh, I don't know, maybe we're wrong."

"Looks like what?"

"Abba, you know how you love to let us see how you are feeling?"

"Yes, Gabriel, I do. My greatest pleasure is to share my heart with those I love. And?"

"Well, when you send us to Luke, I am almost certain that I see you crying."

"Hmmm?"

"Not the great flood of tears you have cried so often, you know, like the way you cry, almost uncontrollably shaking, when you watch a fearful child being abused or when you see refugees fleeing their homeland in unworthy crafts on rough seas."

"Yes, go on, Gabriel."

"Sometimes when you cry, Abba, I cannot watch. I become desperate; it even feels as if you are not in control anymore. My whole being gets tied up in a knot. I cry too, Abba, on the inside. I know how much you love them, and I know you long for them to know that."

"But you think I am not in control?"

No, God, it's just that, well, I get afraid when I see you that way!"

"Does that feeling stay with you a long time?"

"No, it's kind of strange. It's like this fear I have just gets driven away."

"Ah, my love!"

"Yes, Abba. Your love is perfect!" [1 John 4:18]

A gentle wind blew on God and Gabriel, and the pause gave time for both of them to reflect on the depth and breadth and height of this love that drives out fear.

"And Abba . . ."

"Yes?"

"I didn't give the message to Luke yet. You see, I am troubled by this whole process."

"Process? What process?"

"Well, you called Luke when he was very young, I remember. But you didn't call him to meet you on the mountain. Why not?"

"Gabriel, your question is a good one and easy to answer. You see, when I first called Luke, I had already called his father, William."

"William? I don't understand."

"You don't remember William?"

"Well, yes, I do; but no, not really."

"I called William, and it was the beginning of my plan to send you to Luke."

"How's that?"

"For someone to meet me on the mountain, it is always easier if someone down there can show them the way, at least the first few steps."

"Why? Are your instructions not enough?"

"Yes, for some. But I made them all, and something amazing happens when they help each other."

"What happens?"

"First of all, when they help each other, when they love each other, that's when they really start to know how much I love them."

"Yes, I've noticed that."

"You have?"

"Yes."

"What else have you noticed, Gabriel?"

"I've noticed that they don't really like to help each other very much. It seems like they don't love each other."

"God? Abba? Are you crying?"

→ 2 ←

To Love or Not To Love

"Abba, should I go and call Luke?"

"Gabriel, do you remember when I first called Luke?"

"Not really. I'm not very good with dates. Tell me."

"I decided to put Luke in an easy place to begin with. I wanted to give him a good foundation."

"I know, God. You are always thinking about foundations. The rest of us like it better when hearts are moved, when the mind's eye sees clearly, and when hands are motivated to reach out."

"Yes, I love those parts too, but I will get to all that soon enough. First let me tell you about the foundations."

"Luke's foundations?"

"Yes, Luke's. He was born with a mark, a clear mark, which distinguishes him as mine. They all do. But then you already knew that, Gabriel, of course."

"But God, why do they—"

"Hold on, Gabriel. Let me tell the story. You know that I made them all in my image, in my likeness. Just like me. [Genesis 1:27] That makes it easy for me to call them to the mountain because they understand and recognize my voice." [John 10:27]

"Some of them do!"

"They all do, Gabriel, but many choose to ignore me. And many people listen to other voices that have confused them and made them deaf to my voice." [2 Timothy 4:4]

"Why are there some who have never heard your voice?"

5

"Because there is a god of this world who has blinded their eyes and stopped up their ears." [2 Corinthians 4:4]

"Does that have anything to do with you calling Luke to the mountain?"

"Yes, Gabriel, everything! I really want all of them to know me intimately, as you do. Because when they really know me, I share all my ideas with them, and they love it! They love to listen, and they love to obey. They go where I ask them and do the most amazing things in my name. They cast out demons."

"Just like Jesus!"

"And heal the sick and raise the dead . . . And they will go anywhere when I ask them. They even give up their lives for others!"

"You mean they really show that they love each other?" [John 15:13]

"Yes, they really do love each other, and they make sure that all the little ones can come to me." [Mark 10:14]

"Yes, Abba, I know. I have seen it. But why don't they all want to hear your instructions? Listen to your voice? Know you intimately?"

"Their foundations are not well established. Then comes the mountain and a small matter of the threshing floor."

"Huh?"

Confused and full of questions, Gabriel bit his upper lip and lifted his eyes to Abba once more.

"Check on Luke, Gabriel, will you? He is climbing amongst the low clouds today and needed some time alone before I call him again to the summit."

"He looks tired, Abba, a bit flat and despondent. Why is that? He should be happy. He's set for a rendezvous with his wife and children, isn't he?"

"Oh, he is happy. He loves his family dearly. It's one of his surest pleasures, and he is always thanking me for giving them to him. He makes me smile! It really gives me pleasure to see those two together. They are so good for each other—and those two children. He calls them Niel and Isa, but I call them 'Deep' and 'Light.'"

"Why, Abba?"

"Well, Niel reflects his parents' wealth, a deep wealth of experiences, a deep wealth of thought and reflection. His parents have stored up a lot of love for him, they have sought me deeply in many circumstances, and they have found me. They have a deep love for me, and they trust me deeply.

"Their son is the result of the depth of their relationship with me. He too will go deep in his walk with me. He will face challenges and seek to answer complicated questions, and yes, there will be times when he cannot find the light to guide him. Like his father, he will explore the valleys but will always find me when he seeks me with all his heart." [Jeremiah 29:13]

"And what about Isa?"

"Have you seen her eyes, Gabriel? Have you watched her dance? Seen her smile? Heard her sing? She has inherited her light through her mother's spirit. She is light in spirit and light in vision; light is displayed in her and through her—my light, Gabriel. From a young age, she has allowed me to shine through her. That is why she flies, Gabriel. She may be the first angel who doesn't need wings."

"But what if people try to take Niel to the shadowlands? Or try to show Isa the fruits of darkness?"

"Luke has asked me always to keep them full. He has been wise in his asking to fill them with love, joy, peace, patience, kindness, goodness, faithfulness, gentleness, and self-control."

"But Luke is not very patient, is he?"

"No, Gabriel, that's true. But be patient with him."

→3←

To Be or To Climb?

"But why does Luke seem so despondent, God?"

"Gabriel, you know I have been speaking with Luke for a long time, and I am so looking forward to being with him at the top of the mountain."

"Yes, I kind of understood that, God. I just don't get why he takes so long to hear you and climb up."

"Ah, Gabriel, well, even you have something to learn today."

"Huh?"

"It's not really about climbing the mountain; it's about being on the mountain!"

"Being? But how can you be if you don't climb. Abba? Why are you crying again, Abba?"

"I see lots of hurts today, Gabriel. I see lots of pain.[1] So many of my children are looking for me and only encountering sadness. [Luke 21:19] I never stop crying, Gabriel. Sometimes you just don't notice my tears."

Getting To Know the Voice

"Gabriel, do you believe young men can rise up on wings like eagles?" [Isaiah 40:31]

"Oh, yes, Abba!"

"Then why do you get stuck on the idea of the climb?"

"I don't get it."

"Do you remember Moses?"

"Do I remember Moses?" Gabriel was surprised at the question. "You're funny, Abba."

"Do you remember when I called Moses to the mountain?"

"Yes, but which time are you referring to? You called him more than once."

"The time when he met me face-to-face, when my glory shone through him, and his hope became rooted in my glory."

"He was old, Abba! At least by their standards."

"Yes, he was. Did you ever wonder why? Did you ever stop to ask me why Moses took so long to meet me on the mountain? You are very concerned about Luke, always fretting because he hasn't made it to the summit yet."

"Yes, but Moses was Moses!"

"Yes, Gabriel, and Luke is Luke."

"When you think of Moses, where do you picture him?"

"What do you mean?"

"Where did Moses spend his time? Where was he when I called him, when I spoke to him, when I prepared him?"

"Was he on the mountain?"

"No, Gabriel. Try a basket on a river!"

"He was alone."

"Yes, and then there was the desert."

"Oh yes, after he—"

"Or when he was alone in a tent . . . How old was Moses when he met me on the mountain?"

"I don't remember. Shall I Google it? Sorry, Abba, I couldn't resist a little joke!"

"Not bad, Gabriel. So, what are you thinking?"

"A river and a desert are funny places for him to be. Why did that happen?"

"Well, the pathway to the top of the mountain is complicated, and to meet me there, my children really need to know me well. Really know my voice. Really trust in me."

"So you test them?"

"No, I train them."

----

1 Hypomoné (ὑπομονή, -ῆς, ἡ)
https://www.billmounce.com/greek dictionary/hypomone
Definition: patient endurance, 2 Cor. 12:12; Col. 1:11; patient awaiting, Lk. 21:19; a patient frame of mind, patience, Rom. 5:3, 4; 15:4, 5; Jas. 1:3; perseverance, Rom. 2:7; endurance in adherence to an object, 1 Thess. 1:3; 2 Thess. 3:5; Rev. 1:9; ἐν ὑπομονῇ and δι Jπομονῆς, constantly, perseveringly, Lk. 8:15; Rom. 8:25; Heb. 12:1; an enduring of affliction, etc., the act of suffering, undergoing, etc., 2 Cor. 1:6; 6:4

→4←

Shaking the Foundations

"Gabriel, two times I have met Luke on the mountain already. Do you remember?"

"No, God, I never saw him on the top of the mountain with you."

"That's because I didn't meet him at the top."

"Was I there? I don't remember."

"No, it was just Luke and me."

"Was it when Luke visited one of your islands?"

"Yes, he was on the island. Do you remember the question I asked him?"

"Yes, yes, I do! I became really excited when I heard him answer so quickly and with such assurance."

"Then you know that the question was, 'When the foundations of the earth are shaken, who is it that holds the earth together?'" [Psalm 75:3]

"He answered so easily, God, didn't he? He really got it. But does that mean that the earthquake on the island was designed by you to show something to Luke?"

"No, but I am able to accomplish many things with one move of my hand. What I am doing on the island is a story for another day."

"Is Luke in that story, Abba?"

"Hmmm, you ask a lot of questions. Luke asks that one a lot as well. He asked it while he sat there, dejected, on the flat roof overlooking the derelict city, remember?"

"Oh, yes. I love this story!"

"He was really upset. I took him as far as I could that day, but it was more than enough for him. He was very tired, angry, and despondent—like he is today."

"He had reason to be despondent, didn't he, Abba?"

"Yes. He was experiencing first-hand what happens when I shake the foundations."

"And if I remember right, you asked him what the righteous should do when the foundations are being destroyed." [Psalm 11:3]

Gabriel recalled how the brokenness on the island, the despair and sadness, had driven a spear of hopelessness through Luke's heart during those days. The more Abba talked about it, the more Gabriel remembered.

"He had just seen a vision. I sent an angel who opened the gates of Hades and gave him a clear view of the destruction of my worlds."

"Jasmine?"

"Yes, Gabriel. Our precious Jasmine. She presented herself to him with no leg, no home, no father—"

"And no hope," interrupted Gabriel, then he paused and held his breath before releasing it in a short burst. "He saw it, didn't he?"

"Yes, he did. He saw it all, and he cried out to me. From his heart he cried. He sat on the roof and looked at the mountain rising from the turmoil of the city streets, and he knew from where his help would come. [Psalm 127]

"And he knew he needed light to guide his steps. The path he would walk was narrow, and the light enough only for the next step. In fact, on that day, the light was not enough even to see one step ahead."

"You gave him light?" asked Gabriel.

12

"Yes, I heard his cry and gave them Isa."

"But he didn't even set foot on the mountain!"

"No, but I sat with him on that roof."

"And he had no idea that one day he would climb that mountain?"

"No, I didn't tell him. That would be a surprise for another day!"

⇒5⇐

"Run Aways" and "Climb Alones"

"God?"

"Yes, Gabriel?"

"Luke."

"What about him?"

"I didn't call him! We got distracted, Abba, and I didn't call him yet. Oops!"

"You got distracted, Gabriel, but Luke is fine. Do not be anxious about anything, but in everything, even Luke, present your requests to me." [Philippians 4:6]

"But I don't understand."

"Do you feel peace?"

"Yes, funny that!"

"It transcends understanding, doesn't it?" [Philippians 4:7]

"Will you guard Luke's heart and soul, Abba?"

"Yes, he already knows my son well, and that is all the help he needs. He'll be okay for a while if you don't call him just yet. Let me tell you about the mountain."

"The mountain? I thought you were telling me about the foundations?"

"What does a mountain stand on?"

"Ah!"

"You see, Gabriel, many stand at the foot of the mountain and long to go up. But the valley is a strange place. The mountain casts shadows, and if you don't seek the help of my Spirit to guide you, then other spirits will try to turn you away."

"How?"

"Behold though I walk through the valley—"

"Of the shadow of death," interrupted Gabriel.

"I will fear no evil!" finished God. [Psalm 2]

"But they do fear evil."

"Yes, because they have not recognized my voice calling from the mountain."

"What do they do, God, if they haven't recognized your voice?"

"They seek all kinds of solutions. Some of them even try to climb the mountain."

"On their own?"

"Yes, unfortunately, on their own."

"What should they do?"

"Be still."

"Be still and know that you are God!" [Psalm 46:10]

"Lay down."

"Lay down in green pastures?"

"Yes, in any of the green pastures in the valley."

"And do what, Abba?"

"Look to the mountain, because that is where their help will come from." [Psalm 121:1-2]

"But what about those who don't lie down and wait?"

"Well, they divide into three groups. One group that I call 'Run Aways' runs away from the mountain as far as they can. They are shown all sorts of lies and deceptions—all very colorful and attractive—leading deeper into the valley and further from the mountain. The lights are bright and the feelings sharp, but unfortunately, they fade, and the darkness is darker, much darker the further from the mountain they stray."

A pause allowed these heavy words to sink in, and Gabriel thought he felt a shiver down his back.

"But can they come back to the mountain?"

"Oh, yes, any one of the Run Aways can come back at any time. Remember the eagles? Always ready to help the weary." [Exodus 19:4]

"But if they drift away, how can they come back? How will they find their way?"

"Have you ever noticed when you are close to a mountain, it is huge and imposing, the summit enticing. But when you are far away, the vision of the mountain in the distance is often more majestic, wonderful, and magnificent."

"Can they always see it, Abba? Even when they are far, far away?"

"It is very hard to be so far away that you are unable to see the mountain."

"Why don't they all come back then?"

"They think they can't."

"They think they can't, or they don't want to?"

"A mixture really, as they have often been convinced that I no longer love them, that they could never be loved by me. Some of them have been convinced that I don't exist."

"Abba, your tears, it's like your heart is broken!"

"Yes, Gabriel. Yes."

Sometimes Gabriel felt at one with God, as if he were experiencing the same feelings, the feelings of a father looking at the distant horizon after his prodigal son.

"And the others?"

"Yes, Gabriel. You know Run Aways, and I am certain you have met those I call 'Climb Alones.'"

"Climb Alones?"

"Yes, a Climb Alone is one of my greatest sadnesses."

"Why?"

"Because Climb Alone has never understood how much I love him."

16

"I think I know him. I am pretty sure I saw him on the mountain."

"Well, let me ask you something, Gabriel."

"Sure. What is it?"

"What was Climb Alone doing on the mountain?"

"What was he doing? Well, climbing, of course!"

"Are you sure?"

"Yes. Well, no . . . Come to think of it, Climb Alone didn't look very happy."

"What makes you say that?"

"He looked a little unsure of himself, as if he didn't really know which way to go."

"But you said he was climbing?"

"Come to think of it, he looked a little lost."

"Did he ask for help?"

"No, not really. Well, he did ask for things: money, healing, doors to open, blessing, anointing. He even asked for peace in the Middle East."

"But did he ask for help to climb the mountain?"

"No, Abba, funny that, you would think that he would ask for help, especially as he knows you are waiting for him at the top."

"Did he never ask for help?"

"Actually, he did ask one time, and I was going to tell you. But before I could, he had already gone."

"Gone where?"

"Well, first he changed the subject, started just talking about other things . . . "

"You mean he asked for help and didn't wait for the answer?"

"Yes, and he moved."

"He moved?"

"Yes. You always told me that when they get lost, they should stay where they are until someone finds them, until help arrives."

"Oh yes, one of the first lessons I give to fathers! Tell your children to wait where they are if they get lost in a marketplace."

"And he moved the wrong way, God."

"Explain what you mean."

"Well, a bit like David . . . If he wants to see the goodness of the Lord, he should be strong and take heart and wait." [Psalm 31:24]

"Wait for what?"

"Solomon!"

"Wait for Solomon?"

"No, Abba. Wait like Solomon! He knew how to go up the mountain, didn't he?"

"How?"

"He had trust in you. He waited for you, acknowledged you, and didn't try and figure it out on his own. He didn't lean on his own understanding."

"And what happens when a person does that?"

"He will make—no, you will make the path straight!" [Proverbs 3:5-6]

"Exactly!"

➔6↤

Circular Routes and Wisdom

"But God, then something funny happened. I'm a bit embarrassed to tell you."

"Why do you say that?"

Gabriel had momentarily forgotten that Abba was omniscient, and he continued. "Climb Alone did something really strange. It made me a bit uncomfortable, and I didn't really know what to do with myself."

"What happened?"

"Climb Alone was a bit despondent, a bit lost, as I said, when out of the bushes came another climber. They both introduced themselves to each other as 'Climb Alone.' John Climb Alone and David Climb Alone. They seemed pleased to discover that they were related."

"Carry on, Gabriel."

"Then another came, and after a while, there were a number of them—Jane Climb Alone, Val Climb Alone, Tom Climb Alone . . ."

"And this was good?"

"It certainly looked good. They had a really good time together. They sang some songs about soldiers and fighting some sort of good fight and even about needing you. They shared their food and even set up a stage with speakers and microphones in a clearing so that when they spoke and sang, the people in the valley below could hear them."

"Sounds good to me. What made you uncomfortable?"

Gabriel adjusted his wings and shifted his weight to his other foot. "I had been watching them climb, and, well, they all looked like they were lost. But when they were together, they all pretended like they knew the way."

"Pretended?" God asked with a smile.

"That's what it looked like. They didn't share their difficulties. In fact, they all shared how great their climb was. Told stories of wonderful happenings on the way and how much they loved you. But then . . ."

"But then what, Gabriel?"

"Strange. They all left!"

"Left?"

"Yes, each one went a different way, and they all said the same thing."

"What did they say?"

"'See you next week!'"

"Hmmm."

"And they said, 'Same time, same place!'"

"Why is that strange, Gabriel?"

"I think like this . . . If they are trying to go up the mountain to meet with you, then how can they meet at the same place next week?"

"Ahhh!"

"And why, Abba? Why did they need to lie to each other saying they knew the way to the top of the mountain? Each one took a different path. Why didn't they all go together, or at least in pairs or groups?"

"Why?"

"You know God, when two or three are gathered together, and two are stronger than one, and when one falls down and when a cord has three strands . . . Oh, Abba, you know the rest!"

"Gabriel, Gabriel."

"Abba?"

"They are Climb Alones."

"God? Do they always have to climb alone?"

"No, Gabriel. No. It's a choice." [Matthew 18:20; Ecclesiastes 4:9-12]

Under the Shade of the Cedar Tree

"Abba, is Luke a Climb Alone?"

"Sometimes, Gabriel, yes."

"Has he ever been a 'Run Away?'"

"Yes, even now he has a longing for the valley. He thinks that the fruit in the valley is wonderful, and sometimes he can't quite grasp that my fruit is so much sweeter."

"Has he ever tasted your fruit, Abba?"

"Yes, he has, but he forgets and doesn't leave it long enough in his mouth to savor all its goodness."

"What happens when he longs for the valley?"

"He slips."

"He slips?"

"Yes, he is climbing a mountain, and sometimes his foot slips!"

"And you let him slip, God?"

"No, I make his feet firm like the feet of a deer so that he can stand on the heights."

"And his steps hold to your path?"

"Yes. He lifts up his eyes to the hills where I am, and I help him. I won't let his foot slip." [Psalm 18:33; 121:3]

"But, God?"

"Yes, Gabriel."

"I've seen Luke's foot slip!"

"Have you?"

"Yes, even these days. I am certain of it!"

"Gabriel, where is Luke now?"

"I don't know. I haven't been watching him."

"Look. What do you see?"

"It seems like he's doing nothing."

"Look closely, Gabriel."

"Okay . . . Ahhh!"

"What do you see?"

"The branch of an almond tree?"

"Gabriel!"

"A boiling pot tipping away from the north?"

"I am happy to see that you remember the stories of old, Gabriel. But what do you see?"

"I see a cedar tree, Abba."

"Are you sure?"

"Yes, a cedar tree. The most beautiful tree I have ever seen. You know, as wide as it is tall. Wow! What a wonderful tree."

"Where is the tree?"

"Oh, I will never forget where this tree is . . . It's so beautiful."

"Tell me about it, Gabriel."

"It's on the side of the mountain—the rugged, windswept mountain. It is majestic in the way it spreads its limbs equally about its solid trunk."

"Really?"

"Yes, so solid . . . and so wide. It looks like it could never be shaken."

"And Luke? Where is Luke?"

"Oh, I see now! He's there, right up close to the trunk, sitting with his back to the tree, resting, his knees pulled up almost to his chest."

"Resting on the unmovable?"

"Yes, God."

"Trusting in the unshakable?"

"Yes!"

"Pressing into the unwavering?"

"Yes, he is!"

"You said that it is a rugged, windswept mountain?"

"Yes . . . well, windswept is perhaps an understatement. The wind is so strong, and the only place that is not affected by the wind is the backside of the tree, sheltered from the wind and snow."

"I love the snow."

"You should, God, you did make it."

"Yes, I love everything I have made."

⇒ 7 ⇐

Pay Careful Attention

"God?"

"What is it, Gabriel?"

"How can the branches of the tree support the weight of all that snow?"

"The cedar tree holds many secrets. It is strong, stronger than you could imagine, its branches symmetrically arranged to give it balance. Its strength comes from within, deep within."

"Has Luke chosen a good place to rest?"

"Yes, Gabriel, it is the only place to rest on his climb."

"He's climbing already? I don't understand."

"What don't you understand?"

"Well, I didn't . . . I actually didn't, you know, I forgot to call him to the summit. Sorry!"

"I am not limited by you, Gabriel. Even when one of my children is already climbing the mountain, I won't stop calling them. When they hear me call is how they know they are in the right place."

"Like sheep?"

"Yes, my sheep listen to my voice, I know them, and they follow me." [John 10:27]

"Is Luke already climbing?"

"Yes, he has reached an interesting point in his journey, and the cedar tree plays its part."

"Is that so?"

"Yes, if Luke gives careful attention to his ways." [Haggai 1:7]

24

"Ahh, Haggai."

"Yes, a lot like Haggai. Do you remember the story, Gabriel?"

"A little, but please tell me again."

"I have promised to shake the heavens and the earth." [Hebrews 12:26]

"Was it you, Abba, who shook the island?"

"Yes, amongst other examples. I allowed the island to be shaken, but when the earth and all its people shake, it is I who hold the pillars firm." [Psalm 75:3]

"And when the foundations are being destroyed, what should your children do, Abba?"

"They should seek to trust me and to please me. Then I, the Lord their God, will provide their hope, their consolation, and their security." [Psalm 11]

"How can they please you?"

"By seeking me with all their heart." [Jeremiah 29:13; 1 Chronicles 28:9]

"And by climbing the mountain?"

"Yes, but not all can climb the mountain."

"Why is that?"

"Some people think that everyone should climb my mountain, and others think that only a select few have been chosen to go up."

"Which is true, God? Please tell me. I have always been intrigued."

"Neither is true, Gabriel. Remember, as I have always said, and as I sent my Son Jesus to show them, I am the way, the truth, and the life. No one comes to the top of the mountain but by the way—my Son, Jesus." [John 14:6]

"The shepherd's voice, that's the way!" said Gabriel. "They just have to listen to his voice."

"Not exactly, Gabriel. There's more to it than that. Remember Judas?"

"Yes, I do. Why do you ask?"

"Judas knew the voice of Jesus."

"Ahhhh!"

"But he did not go up the mountain to meet with me."

"Why, God? What really happened to Judas?"

"He heard my voice, but like the foolish man who built his house on the sand, he heard my words and did not put them into practice."

"The moment the torrent struck, God?"

"Destruction was complete." [Luke 6:46-49]

"What about Luke? Has he heard your voice?"

"Oh yes, yes, many times. He knows my voice very well."

"What's his problem then?"

"Problem?"

"Yes, Luke seems to spend so much time looking back down the mountain."

Gabriel was expecting a response, but God remained silent.

→ 8 ←

Daddy! Come Home!

"God? Abba? Abba?"

"What, Gabriel?"

"What happened, Abba? You stopped talking."

"Yes, another father just turned his back on his family, another teenage boy became acutely aware of the infinite warfare, as if it were his call of duty. The last guardian, his father, has left his post. He has begun a new life, like a final fantasy, accompanied only by dark souls, playing into the hands of Diablo, the reaper of souls.[1]

Abba then pointed to a five-year-old girl.

"And that little girl loves her daddy and believes there are only two superheroes in the universe—God and her daddy. The father has a special job to do in the life of his little girl, and as you will have observed, as she grows, she will discover that her daddy is not actually a superhero."

"I don't get it, Abba. What do you mean?"

"There will come a time when the little girl grows up and recognizes that her hero father is actually beset with failure and weakness. But when she realizes this truth, a good father should already have presented his daughter to me."

"And you really are a superhero, Abba!"

"You make me smile, Gabriel. Actually, a surer hope than any superhero."

"I get it, I think. The father has a job to do, to keep his son safe from the attacks of Diablo, to protect him."

"Exactly. As a prophet," said God.

"To guide him in paths of righteousness so that he too can climb the mountain to meet with you?" asked Gabriel.

"Yes, the role of a priest."

"As well as being a prophet and a priest in his home."

Gabriel, excited, wanted God to know how much he enjoyed investigating life ideas through their conversations.

"Oh, I do so enjoy spending time in your presence, God. Things become so much clearer when we talk."

Then God gently drew Gabriel back into the point of the discussion.

"Yes, Gabriel. You were saying, 'as well as being a prophet and a priest.'"

"Ahhh, yes, Abba, a king!"

"A king?"

"Yes, a king! The father is raising his daughter as a princess until she can see you clearly and begin to understand how your kingdom works. Then she will know how to behave like a princess, the daughter of the true King."

"That's it, Gabriel."

"But there's more, God, isn't there? The father should love his wife as a king loves his queen and cherish his family as a king cares for his kingdom. If he can love her, his wife, as you love your church, then his son will learn to love the same way. His daughter will joyfully prepare for her wedding, and the son will become enthralled at the possibility of building his family. And the bride and the bridegroom will have an encounter at the conclusion of time. It's a beautiful picture, Abba. Family!"

"Yes, yes, it is. If only the fathers would come home." [Ephesians 5:25; Revelation 19:7]

---

[1]Infinite Warfare, Call of Duty, Final fantasy, Dark Souls, Diablo, Reaper of Souls. Popular video game titles.

→ 9 ←

Clean Hands and Pure Hearts

"Abba?"

Yes, Gabriel?"

"Why does Luke spend so much time looking back down the mountain?"

"Because he is stuck."

"How is he stuck?"

"Do you remember the story of my prophet Haggai? I sent him to speak with Zerubbabel."

"Yes, I remember, but why do you ask about Haggai?"

"I told him to give careful thought to his ways, to go up the mountain. [Haggai 1:7-8] Do you remember what I told them to do? Seek to please me."

Gabriel tilted his head before exclaiming, "That was always your plan with your Son, Jesus, wasn't it?"

"Yes! Jesus, my Son, whom I love and in whom I am well pleased."

Both God and his angelic companion smiled knowingly at the thought of such a simple, uncluttered objective.

"Gabriel, how should they, my children, begin to climb the mountain to meet with me? How should they ascend the mountain of the Lord?"

With eyes wide open and an eyebrow raised, Gabriel hesitated and answered God's question with a question. "Only the one who has clean hands and a pure heart, who does not trust in an idol or swear by a false God, can climb?" [Psalm 24:4]

"Yes, Gabriel, well done."

"What then?"

"Imagine if you are already on the mountain, climbing to meet with me, and you suddenly stop and look down at your hands. You see that they are not clean. And imagine if you look back at what your hands have tried to build, and you don't see anything. Or worse, what if you see what you have built, but you are not satisfied with the work of your hands?"

"Discouragement, Abba? Is that why Luke keeps looking back down the mountain? Is Luke discouraged?"

"Yes, he is. Luke feels that his heart is not pure, his hands are not clean, and he has considered letting idols into his life."

"Idols? Tell me that's not true!"

"Yes, the idols of success, reward, esteem, and recognition. Diablo knows Luke's heart, and he continually tries to tempt him."

"But Luke seems so strong and self-confident."

"Do you really think so, Gabriel?"

Gabriel rested his forefinger on his lips and responded thoughtfully, "Come to think of it, he has been a little unsure on his feet. He says it's his fear of heights. But it's not that, is it?"

"No, it's not fear of heights. It's his pride, which is why his foot slips, and I have to draw his attention once more to me."

"Pride?"

"Yes, sometimes he calls it a mid-life-crisis."

"Yes, I've heard him say that a lot recently."

"But Luke has always tended to let his foot slip. Because he loves to look down to where he has been and not look up to where he is going."

"Where has he been, Abba?"

"He's been to many places—some you have heard of, some maybe not. He has been to Thrill, where he stayed with the

Osophers and spent time with Chance and Luck. He has been to Wisdom's house and met Idealist, Materialist, and Hegelian. Reason has been his companion, and he has been utterly confused in the presence of both Lust and Shame."

Sister Hope Points the Way

"Luke has traveled a lot, hasn't he, Abba."

"Yes, he has, and like so many of his compatriots, he has traveled further still and discovered the homes of Pain, Abuse, and Deception. But finally, in the Valley of Despair, sitting by a small brook, I found him, idly chatting with Sister Hope and dismissing almost every word of cheer she had to say. A gash of rejection pierced his heart along with the belief that this valley would forever be his home."

"How did he get out of the valley, Abba?"

"He still visits the valley from time to time. But I do believe he is finally seeing the futility of returning to the valley. I believe he is ready to enter the unshakable kingdom."

"But how did he get out of the valley, away from despair? How did the gash of rejection heal?"

"It is a process. The wound across his heart has been slow to heal, and it is still not closed completely. At times I must send my spirit to lay across his heart and bind him up one more time. The spirit's tears heal, and Jesus, my Son, intercedes for him."

"Will it ever heal completely?"

"Why do you ask? You know I am Jehovah Rapha!" [Exodus 15:26]

"Yes, but I see so many of your children holding on to pain and hurt as if they cannot or do not want to let it go. Why do they do that?"

"Fear. And while they try to run from their fear, or ignore it, pretend it doesn't exist, or even replace it with temporary victories, experiences, or conquests in their physical and emotional worlds, they will always be blinded to the truth by the god of this world."

"That's where your perfect love comes in handy?"

"Yes! I can drive out all fear, all rejection, all pain, all deception—things that cut, scratch, and strangle their tender hearts."

⇒10⇐

The Valley of Despair

"And what about Luke?"

"I first found Luke in the Valley of Despair when he was 13 years old. He had no idea where he was, and those around him were blind to the dangers. There's a lot of blindness amongst the Climb Alones. They sometimes put blindfolds over their own eyes so that they cannot see."

"You mean they choose to be blind?"

"Yes, and very often they don't even take off their blindfolds when they meet. Sometimes they even make jokes such as 'the blind leading the blind' and are happy about it!"

"Ah, yes, I've seen it, Abba. Then one of them, usually the one in the front, does one of those 'big' sins—that's what they call them, isn't it?"

"Oh, yes. The big sins. And somehow, they all take off their blindfolds just long enough to catch a glimpse of the big sin as it passes by, long enough to judge and pour scorn and condemnation."

"But not long enough to see their own sin?"

"No, and not long enough for them to gaze on my beauty, my perfection, and my love like David did. If they could clearly see me, then they would know that I love them dearly, and I am always ready to forgive their sins and lift them up to sit with me in the high places."

"So how do you get them to come up out of the Valley of Despair?"

"I show them something special."

"What is it?"

"Something tailor-made. They were all fearfully and wonderfully made by me, so I know them all intimately. Deeply. Secretly." [Psalm 139:14]

"Is that what happened to Luke?"

"Yes. I had already softened his heart towards children, and I continue to do so today. I gave him a window into my heart, let him see with my eyes, let him cry my tears for the first time."

"How, Abba? Tell me!"

"I took him on a journey to see Josaña in the Mid-Lands."

"Abba, was Luke's Valley of Despair in the Mid-Lands? I thought he was born in the Far North?"

"Yes, born in the Far North of Celtic blood and mountain heritage. His family migrated to the New Lands, where his story would unfold. In the Near-North, his Valley of Despair began. In the Mid-Lands, he met with Sister Hope for the first time. In the South-Lands, his journey to the top of the mountain will be completed."

"In the Mid-Lands he met someone called Josaña?"

"Yes, Luke was young, Josaña younger still. Their meeting was by my design. I had been crying over Josaña for five years and over Luke only recently . . ."

"Abba?"

"Josaña was an orphan, and Luke had a broken heart. Josaña did not break it, but she found an easy way in through the gash of mistrust and confusion. And there she stayed and stays."

"I don't really get it. Tell me more. What did Luke see, Abba?"

"That was exactly my question too, and that was the first time I asked him what he saw."

"Did he answer your question?"

"Yes. Through his tears he saw me, and he knew that to heal his heart, he would need to trust me and let me teach him how to love Josaña—how to love an orphan."

"Or maybe how to be a sheep and not a goat?"

"Yes, Gabriel, good cross-referencing!" [Matthew 25:31-46]

"But Luke was so young. How could he feed her, clothe her? He was already wearing hand-me-downs."

"You're right, Gabriel. But on that day, he began. What he had, he gave her—a balloon and a hug. And his heart he gave to me."

"Diablo has tried and tempted, but Luke has always returned to me."

"But sometimes he takes so long to come back."

"Yes, he is a bit slow at times, but he always returns, and I remind him of Josaña and help him to take his eyes off the valley below."

Too Ill To Climb

"Abba, when Luke is sitting beneath the branches of a cedar tree, two thousand feet up the side of a windswept, snow-blown mountain, what does he see in the valley below?"

"He sees many things, and he thinks he sees many more."

"But what does he see?"

"He sees all the people he has met, all the things he has done, all the dreams, all the conquests, and all the successes. And, he sees all the failures."

"Failures?"

"Yes. Sadly, he sees his failures very clearly. In fact, those are the clearest images in his mind's eye."

"The clearest images are of his failures? Why?"

"He has a common ailment, Gabriel."

"Is Luke ill?"

"Yes, I am afraid so."

"Can he be healed?"

"Rapha, Gabriel. R-A-P-H-A!"

Gabriel smiled to himself as he once again realized he had forgotten to take into consideration the nature of the one to whom he was talking!

"What's making him sick?"

"It's not only Luke. So many of them have the same condition."

"What do you mean, Abba? What condition do they suffer from?"

"As they go on their journeys, they choose their traveling companions. They are wise when they ask me first whom they should travel with. They are wise when they recognize the nature of the climb ahead and realize, early on, that they are ill-equipped for the ascent if they tackle it alone."

"What do you mean?"

"It's like this, Gabriel. The beginning of wisdom is to get wisdom. Though it cost you all you have, get understanding." [Proverbs 4:6-7]

"Solomon, then, was wise because he asked for wisdom. And what about Luke?"

"Yes, Luke too. He also asked for wisdom, and he has been given a good measure."

"What's the problem?"

"The wisdom that comes from heaven is first of all pure, then peace-loving." [James 3:17]

"And Luke's wisdom isn't pure?"

"The problem is that when Luke looks at his hands, he doesn't see them as clean, and when he reflects on the state of his heart, he questions his purity."

"Why?"

"Because he has allowed his pure, peace-loving wisdom to be contaminated."

"Contaminated by what?"

"During his climb, when he was a good way along the pathway of contentment, he stopped. He stopped and took a wrong turn and went to visit Comparison's house."

Gabriel let out a knowing sigh.

"He saw Comparison's family, listened to Comparison's stories, and set them on the mantle next to his own."

"But surely wisdom carried him back quickly to the path?"

"Yes, but Luke had already decided to carry with him some of Comparison's belongings."

"But didn't Luke realize that Comparison has his struggles, his challenges? Did Luke only take with him those things that weigh him down?"

"Yes, Gabriel, there are days when Luke and so many others, especially the Climb Alones, spend so much of their energy looking at the things they took from Comparison's house that they grow extraordinarily tired."

"But Lord, when they measure themselves by themselves and compare themselves with themselves, they are not wise." [2 Corinthians 10:12]

"Yes, Gabriel, I know."

"Why don't they just look at you?"

"You mean just gaze on my beauty?"

"Yes."

"Because on the climb, when their foot slips, they look down, not up."

"Is it so hard for them to see that you always keep them safe in the day of trouble, hide them in your shelter, and set them high upon a rock?" [Psalm 27]

"Until they meet me on the mountain, it is hard for them, yes. Diablo makes it hard, and they keep remembering that they already fell once, which makes them more aware of the possibility of falling again. They believe not falling is impossible. They give up instead of looking up."

"But surely once they have caught a glimpse of you, Abba, then they gain strength and hope?"

"Yes, yes, they do. It's always a special moment when one of my children catches a glimpse of me for the first time and calls out, 'Abba!'"

"Then why can't they always look up?"

"Because they trust the wrong people."

"Who? Who do they trust?"

"Take that busybody, Self-Pity, who is always stepping in to hold the hand of those who have just left Comparison's house."

"I saw Luke talking to Self-Pity the other day."

"Yes, I know. They have become good friends, I am afraid. But not to worry, he has heard my voice again and has begun to lift his head. Have you noticed?"

Gabriel looked towards Luke's shady refuge and saw that he appeared refreshed.

"But the cedar has not finished its work yet. Let him rest some more, Gabriel. Old Self-Pity cannot cope when people lift their heads. Self-Pity always requires full attention. She has a minimal vocabulary and difficulty in maintaining a conversation. Listen."

Both Abba and Gabriel strained to hear the weak, trembling voice of old Self-Pity, who was busy convincing a Climb Alone of his needs and rights.

"Oh yes, Abba, I noticed already and made a mental note to ask you why she only repeats those same words?"

"All other words scare her, Gabriel. 'There-there, dear' and 'Look at me, look at me' and 'You'll be okay if you keep looking at me' are the words of old Self-Pity. She'll take them to her grave with her!"

→ 11 ←

Planting Much for Little Return

"God, when I look at Luke, back against the cedar, I see him rub his eyes. He does it again and again, and his breathing slows. They are deep breaths, but the release is slow and hard, accompanied by a slight shake of the head. He pinches the bridge of his nose between forefinger and thumb and grabs a handful of hair in his hand as if to pull it out."

God, knowing a question is coming, raised his eyebrows and asked Gabriel to go on. "Hmmm?"

"What is he thinking about, Abba?"

"His body is reacting."

"Reacting to what?"

"To the smarting hand of disappointment."

"But there's no one else near him."

"Consider disappointment being like walking into the teeth of the North Wind," God said, wringing his hands as if he were feeling the cold. "The wind brings the bitter cold as disappointment swipes across the heart with a sharp blow designed to reach in and stir up all the emotions held deep within."

"Oh, no, Abba. Luke already carries the scar of rejection in his heart. Can he cope with disappointment too?"

"No, Gabriel, he can't. No one can. I didn't make my children like that. I gave them tender hearts, new spirits, hearts of flesh." [Ezekiel 36:26]

"But if their hearts were made of stone, then disappointment and rejection would not hurt them."

"You are right, but without a tender heart they could never learn forgiveness. And without forgiveness, they will never experience unconditional love."

Memory and Expectation

"What about Luke's disappointment? Why does he carry such deep feelings?"

"Well, for all who decide to visit Comparison's house and walk with Self-Pity, Disappointment is never too far away. Disappointment whispers from the tangled weeds beside the path and plays games called Memory and Expectation."

"Those are games?"

"Yes, there are simple rules for Disappointment's games. But they are not my rules."

"So, what are the rules then, Abba?"

"First, you must make a list of memories, but you must always have at least two bad or sad memories for every good or happy one. Whenever a good memory comes up, you must quickly cover it with the two bad memories to not create what Disappointment calls false expectations."

"False expectations?"

"In my family, we call it hope, Gabriel."

"Oh, yes, I love hope!"

"So do I. So do I."

"And hope deferred makes the heart sick, doesn't it ?" [Proverbs 13:12]

"Yes, that's why Disappointment always has some pills or a stiff drink at hand for those who visit Comparison and spend time with Self-Pity. His cousin, Depression, keeps him amply supplied with free samples.

"Disappointment, you see, knows exactly what he is doing. On the climb, it is easy to become weary. There are enough challenges to make simply hearing my voice and keeping to the narrow path difficult. When my children pause to consider other voices, though, like Disappointment's, then their mind becomes drawn to Diablo's value system that uses a completely different vocabulary to the one I use."

"Like false expectations?"

"Yes! And they listen to Highly-stressed, Deeply-anxious, Sort-of', Could-be, and Maybe-so."

"I am almost certain I have seen Sort-of, Could-be, and Maybe-so on the mountain. They're Climb Alones, aren't they?"

"Yes, Gabriel, they are very talented Climb Alones. They have perfected the art of climbing in circles."

"How's that, God, I mean climbing in circles?"

"Whenever you climb and end up at the same place you began, you will almost always encounter those three scoundrels, Gabriel."

"Why do you call them scoundrels?"

"They are always sowing seeds of doubt in the minds of earnest climbers. When asked directions, instead of pointing the climber in my direction, Sort-of and his companions always answer the same way, "Is this the right way, friend?" is the question and "Could-be!" the reply.

"So, off the would-be climber goes in yet another circular climb. Maybe-so and Sort-of are so wise in their own eyes that they truly believe they can shed light on any subject."

"Instead of letting their yes be yes, and their no be no? Instead of urging the climber to seek you with all their heart?" [Matthew 5:37]

"Yes, Gabriel. Diablo has them doing his dirty work."

"What about the Climb Alones? Do they understand all this?"

"Understand what?"

"That if they were to seek you with all their heart, they would find you, and they don't need the guesswork of the three know-it-alls?"

"Yes, Gabriel, they know that they will find me. They know that I will gather them from all nations when they seek me." [Jeremiah 29:13-14]

"And what about Luke? Did his hope die?"

"No, not exactly. But Disappointment took Luke by the hand and reminded him of his past."

"And that caused a problem?"

"Yes, he feels he has planted much for little return, and this has saddened him."

"Little return? You mean he has harvested little?" [Haggai 1:6]

"He forgets my story sometimes, Gabriel."

"And he thinks he is writing the story on his own?"

"Yes, something like that."

→12←

The Mother of All Lies!

"Abba, you said that sometimes Luke forgets your story."

"Yes, many of them like to embellish my story to make it more manageable, more palatable, easier to swallow and . . ."

"And what, Abba?"

"You see, Gabriel, I gave the climbers some guidelines, helped them put things in order. [Genesis 1:26-27] I made them this way. They are like us. The climbers like to be able to see how everything is connected, to discover new secrets and see how they are related to the secrets they already discovered!"

God paused as if collecting his thoughts.

Gabriel, impatient, interjected, "So? God?"

"Take Luke, for example. He knows full well the guidelines and laws I have established for his well-being, and he is good at keeping most of them, but I always want them to see beyond the laws."

"To know you for who you are!"

"Yes, Gabriel, the laws are there to help them, but beyond the law . . . where I am—"

"I don't see, Abba," Gabriel interrupted again.

"Don't see what?"

"What you are trying to say. Because you said that everyone should love you and love their neighbor as they love themselves."

"Yes, that is the law." [Mark 12:30-31]

"But then you said, 'These three things remain: faith, hope, and love."

As Gabriel took a breath, God asked him, "And which of these is the greatest?"

"Love! So, Abba, where is the problem? I don't get it."

God smiled knowingly and with a slight nod of his head, said, "Gabriel, when my children look at the law, they see it as an end, not a means."

Gabriel, more baffled than ever, scratched his head.

"And," God continued, "they begin to add conditions to the law. First, they categorize my law into possible and impossible."

"Possible and impossible?" asked Gabriel.

"Yes, they think it is reasonable and possible not to take another's life. But they consider it unreasonable and impossible not to covet their neighbors' possessions."

"Yes, you're right, God! I never thought about it like that."

"The climbers also consider it possible not to steal but impossible and impractical to have no other God besides me."

Gabriel was shocked and exclaimed, "No, I've never heard them say that!"

"I know. They have a problem with truth-telling as well."

"What do they do, Abba? Everything you are telling me is so confusing to me."

"They make lists and tables."

Lists and Tables

"I don't understand," said Gabriel.

"They use lists and tables to classify themselves according to the law."

"How do these lists work?

God stretched slightly and leaning on the doorframe, easing into his explanation. "Like this: they make a list of my laws and the conditions of when my laws should be applied. They choose their favorite parts of the law, and they organize their life so that others can see them obeying the most visible of these important laws."

"Oh, that is interesting."

"You think so? That's what they say!"

Gabriel shook his head. "I'm still a bit confused, Abba."

"Just as they are, Gabriel. That's why they need the tables to help them make sense of the lists. Let me explain. The tables are charts of success and failure. If you do well according to the published list that your group of Climb Alones has agreed upon, then you are considered successful in obedience to my law. And if you are successful, you gain kudos and status and become well-regarded amongst your group, and often even with other similar groups."

"Wow, so they promote themselves according to their success with your law."

God smiled wryly. "Not exactly. It's more complicated than that because they have various mechanisms for gaining status. You see, following the law can become tedious and difficult, just like climbing."

"So, what do they do, Abba?"

"When they are climbing, at times the route I choose for them is difficult. It is not because I want them to suffer or struggle, but because I really want them to see the view from a certain point. There are some fantastic things to see on the climb."

"But if it is so difficult, isn't it understandable that they choose a different path?"

"It would be understandable if it weren't for the lie."

Gabriel was intrigued and quickly asked, "The lie?"

"Yes, when Diablo first lied to them, he sowed a seed, a seed that is born from a lie and gives birth only to lies."

"What do you mean?"

"Gabriel, you belong to your Father." [Isaiah 43:1]

"I know, Father, and I am so glad!"

"All of them belong to their father, Gabriel."

"Why then is your voice not clear to them?"

"Because they are unable to hear what I say. They belong to their father, Diablo, and they want to carry out his desires. [John 8:44]. I am the one who put this desire in them to follow their father's voice."

Gabriel was beginning to understand.

God continued. "Diablo was a murderer from the beginning, not holding to the truth, for there is no truth in him. When he lies, he speaks his native language, for he is a liar and the father of lies." [John 8:44]

"But why don't they follow you, Father?"

"He who belongs to me hears what I say. The reason they do not hear is that they do not belong to me."

"Oh, Abba, is that true? They say they belong to you, especially when they are together."

"The father of lies, Gabriel, the father of lies."

In a moment of silence, Gabriel swallowed hard as he thought about all those climbers who pretended to be on the right path but who had never truly heard Abba's voice. A tear slid down his cheek.

"God, pardon the pun, but saying they belong to you when they don't recognize your voice seems like the mother of all lies."

"Gabriel, give me a few moments alone, would you? I need to spend some time with Luke."

⇢13⇠

Faith, Hope, Love, and Comparison

"Abba, can I ask you something?"

"Yes, Gabriel, of course."

"When we last talked, you told me about the law, the lists, and the tables . . . and the people who were choosing the less difficult path."

Abba nodded and said, "When they look at the path I have chosen for them, they sometimes shudder!"

"Why?"

"Yes, because they cannot see beyond the first step. They hope they will reach their goal—"

"But Diablo lies!" Gabriel interrupted.

"Yes, and he plays the memory game with them."

"Telling them that their hope is just a false expectation?"

"Yes, Gabriel, that's exactly what happens. For those who take the first step, to their hope is added faith, and when the next step is hard to see, faith carries them forward and renews their hope."

Gabriel, in need of a more detailed explanation, raised his eyebrows.

God asked, "Have you seen that invention of theirs, the bicycle?"

"Yes."

"Remember the old-fashioned lights called dynamos?"

Gabriel flashed a smile of recognition. "Yes, I do. What a clever invention! The more you pedal, the more light you generate, and the more light you generate, the more you can see, and the more you can see, the more you want to keep going. You pedal more—faith—and you see more—hope."

Abba's gentle smile was one of a teacher satisfied with his student's answer.

"Oh, but . . ." Gabriel said disheartened.

"What, Gabriel?"

"God, it seems that they would only have to exercise their faith one time to realize it works, and then they would always want to keep going. So why do they stop? Why do they turn around? Why don't they follow your voice?"

"Gabriel, we just talked about faith and hope, but what is missing?"

Gabriel, perfectly capable of a quick response, hesitated, wondering if the question was a trick.

"Love, Abba?"

"Love. Yes, Gabriel. Remember the father of lies? There is only one way to defeat him—love."

"How?"

"You see, the Climb Alones are always having to choose between the lists and tables and love."

Confused, Gabriel waited for Abba to continue.

"When they approach the law, they categorize themselves. Remember? They use their table of success and failure to generate kudos and status. For example, somebody who regularly gives large tithes and offerings and makes it publically known through the tables gains great kudos. In contrast, one who wears shorts and sandals to their meetings is frowned upon and falls down the table."

"Is that how it works?" Gabriel asked, listening intently.

"Yes. Funnier still, if the one who wears shorts and sandals instead of more formal attire also gives generously to the poor, but does not record his generosity in the table, he will still fall to the lower reaches of the table because of a lack of published data."

"Wow! But God, doesn't humility come into play? Didn't you say that the right hand should not know what the left hand is doing?" [Matthew 6:3]

"Yes, that is how it should work, but remember, so many of them have been guests in Comparison's house."

A light came on in the young angel's head.

"Comparison! Of course, he must just love the lists and tables."

"Yes, Gabriel, very much so. And there are others involved as well."

"Others? Who?" said Gabriel.

"They are not very subtle. When they achieve success according to their position in the tables, they receive medals and prizes."

"Who gives them medals and prizes?"

"Some of Diablo's best henchmen."

A thought flashed through Gabriel's mind, and he said, "Are you telling me that they make these lists and tables at their meetings? But isn't that when they are publically giving glory to you, singing your praises, and seeking to learn more of you, together?"

God's smile told a story, and he replied gently, "Yes, Gabriel, a bit of a mess. Many of them do meet with me in those encounters, but others take along Pride and Selfishness, which makes the encounters less than pleasant."

"Who are Pride and Selfishness?"

"They live in Comparison's house, and they help to create and publish the tables."

The Four Choices

"Abba, in their tables, someone must always be at the bottom. You know, someone who has a hard time keeping all the laws on the list or fails more often than the others."

"Good observation. Often those who struggle the most realize they need help. When they realize they can't climb the table on their own, they often start to listen to my voice and follow me."

"That's funny, Abba."

"Why do you say that?"

"You would think that following you would be their first choice; after all, you did make them!"

"When they know me, they always follow me, because to know me is to love me and be loved by me."

Astutely aware of details picked up on what he thought was a flaw in Abba's explanation, Gabriel said, "You said often. Why not always?"

"What do you mean?

"You said, 'When they realize they can't climb the tables on their own, they often start to listen to my voice and follow me.' Why didn't you say always?"

"Remember when I told you about Comparison's house?"

"Yes, I remember."

"And on leaving Comparison's house, they walk for a while with Self-Pity?"

"Yeah."

"Well, on the way, Self-Pity often shows them a trick. She has always tried to cut corners and avoid dealing with her fears, and for a time, she dabbled in magic, but there was one trick she managed to perfect."

Gabriel was intrigued. "What trick?"

"It's a little bit like the memory game. For every good

memory, cover it up with two bad ones, remember?"

"Oh, yes, Abba, so what is this new trick?"

"The memory game focuses on self, but this trick focuses on others. Where the memory game draws you into depression and despair, this trick takes you down a shortcut on your climb and looks like it will take you straight to the top of the mountain. Straight to kudos and status."

"Tell me how it works, God."

"When you perceive that you are failing to live up to the pre-set standards of the lists, and when you believe, or even see, that your name is slipping down the table, you find yourself with a series of choices—four to be exact.

"The first and best choice, which leads to life and life in abundance, is to follow me. Those who follow do so because they know my voice." [John 10:27,10]

"Yes, and those who don't know you will run away because they don't know your voice?" [John 10:4-5]

"Yes, that is the second choice, run so far away that they become lost forever. But others choose one of two paths . . ."

Gabriel knew that he needed to pay careful attention, so he shuffled his feet and leaned against the doorpost beside him.

"Some rely on their strength, talents, and understanding, working hard to achieve more and more, dining often with Pride and missing out on precious moments with their children and the rest of their families." [Proverbs 3:5-6]

"You mean they don't submit to you?"

"Right, they become wise in their own eyes."

"And you can't help them keep their paths straight?"

"No, I can't. It makes me very sad because when love and faithfulness are written on their hearts, when they remember my teachings and trust in me with all their heart, then they win my favor. And I give them peace and prosperity because I love

51

them. When they rely on their strength, they may experience success, but what they conquer by their hand simply aids them in their circular climb. To reach the top of the mountain, where I am, however, they are unable."

"But that is only three choices. What is the fourth choice? Is it the trick? Does Luke know about the trick?"

"Patience, Gabriel, patience." Abba chuckled, amused to see his young companion so involved in these deep thoughts.

"Luke?" repeated Gabriel.

"Yes, he knows the trick."

"And does he use it often?"

"Sometimes, yes. But Luke knows it makes me sad."

"Will you tell me about the trick?"

"Reluctantly, yes. It is one of my least favorite of Diablo's games."

→14←

A Twist in the Tail

"I'm sorry, Abba."

"What for?"

"I am sorry that you have to watch your children make such a mess of your wonderful creation."

"Me too, Gabriel, but don't get too discouraged. The story has a twist and a wonderful ending."

"I know, God. And the funny thing is that Diablo knows how it all ends, yet he still keeps trying to stop them from climbing your mountain!"

⇒15⇐

Shortcut to the Summit

"God, will Luke make it to the top of the mountain?"

"Do you mean, is he destined to meet me at the top?"

"Yes, is he destined to reach the summit?"

"Gabriel, I know how the story ends. I know how Luke's story ends, but he still has many choices to make along the way, and he can use many different resources to help him decide the path he will take."

"Sometimes, I see him weeping, Abba, as he considers his choices."

"Yes, and as he talks to me and listens to my voice, I will bring him back; and as he climbs, I will lead him by streams of water on a level path where he will not stumble." [Jeremiah 31:9]

"But Abba, you said there is a trick? The fourth choice?"

"Yes, it is a foolish way that leads you to believe you will arrive at the top of the mountain more quickly."

"Is that possible, Abba?"

"No, it's not possible."

"So why do they learn the trick?"

"Because they have a burning desire to be first, to win, as if climbing the mountain were a race."

"Being first is a bit silly, isn't it?"

"Yes, it is. But they will learn. Slowly, painfully at times, it seems. But when they fall in love with me, they quickly see that the last will be first and the first will be last! [Matthew 20:16]

"So, how does the trick help them?"

Abba folded his arms and lifted his head ever so slightly, and sighed. "When they analyze themselves according to the tables, and when they see that others around them are succeeding by the same measurement scale, they have to make a choice, remember?"

"Yes, you said they could run away and pretend that your commands, your precepts, your instructions are of no relevance."

Under his breath, Gabriel added as if revealing a secret, "Although I notice that they manage to obey a good number of your laws even while denying your existence."

"Yes, Gabriel. They call it common sense. I call it conscience."

"Or they can try and work hard with their gifts and talents, which you gave them, to fight their way to the top by sheer effort and by leaning on their understanding, the second choice you described."

"Yes, or acknowledge me, and I will show them the way to the top of the mountain."

"But the fourth choice, what is it?"

"It's the basis of all wars, the foundation of all things unstable and worthless, the strategy upon which failure is a certainty."

"What is it, Abba?"

"Psithurismós."

Hot Sweet Tea and a Log Fire

"Psithurismós, you mean gossip!" exclaimed Gabriel.

"Remember that well-lit parlor in Comparison's house? The one with the open hearth, log fire, and comfortable armchairs?"

"Uh-huh."

"Do you also recall that cakes and hot sweet tea always accompanied the conversations that took place in that room?

"Yes, it looked so inviting. I wanted to go in for a closer look."

"Yes, Gabriel, I noticed."

"But you called me back quickly, Abba, why?"

Nodding, God said, "Did you notice who was in the parlor?"

"No, not really. Who was there?"

"Comparison doesn't usually sit with his guests but continues to serve them with copious amounts of sweets."

"And?"

"And then he leaves them to chat amongst themselves."

"About what?"

"Usually there are two or three invited to the parlor, individuals who have found some challenges on the climb that are rather daunting. The lists have confronted them, and they have found themselves in the nether regions of the table—or at least they have come to believe they are second-rate climbers and others are doing somewhat better."

"So, what happens?" Gabriel was eager to hear all the details.

"Comparison throws a name into the conversation, an icebreaker he calls it, and suggests that this Other person may not necessarily have achieved his or her success in an altogether appropriate manner . . . Then, as Comparison leaves the room, the guests begin to speak, in gentle words, of course, about the peculiar circumstances by which Other came by his success."

"Wow!"

"They notice that Other has done, or maybe not done, something important that had it been left to them, would have been solved in an instant. They question whether Other's success could be attributed to him at all, or whether it was by way of an inheritance or even by underhanded means that he had achieved such status. They can find any number of occurrences in Other's life that are questionable, none of which they would ever contemplate."

"What an amusing conversation. But what in heaven's name does it accomplish?"

"Nothing. In the minds of the guests, they have merely exchanged ideas and discussed relevant topics in the most delightful of settings."

"And will they ever share their thoughts and feelings about their findings with Other?"

"No, sadly, they won't," said Abba with a shake of his head.

"So, what was the purpose of their conversation?"

"As they leave the parlor, Comparison slips a piece of paper into their pockets."

Intrigued, the young angel asks, "What words are on the paper?"

"They read it as they stroll along the path together. It is what they consider very enjoyable reading."

"Why, God, why?"

"Because it is the new table compiled by Pride and Selfishness which the Climb Alones use for their weekly analysis of the lists."

"What does the new list show?"

"The guests notice that they have all risen one place in the table."

"How did that happen?"

"Very simply. As they spoke about Other and discovered things about him that were not exactly as they had appeared, slowly he slipped—not one, not two, but three places down the table to exactly one place below the three guests."

"Wow. How incredible!"

"Yes!"

"So, they did nothing to merit rising on the table?"

"Nothing."

Wide-eyed, Gabriel pieced together what had happened. "They created doubt about Other so that in the minds of those listening, he was unable to justify such a lofty placing in the table. And they left the parlor feeling good, confident, and ful-filled—a good afternoon's conversation in pleasant surroundings that cost nothing and yet brought about a delightful personal benefit."

"Exactly, Gabriel. All at the cost of Other."

→16←

Further Encounters with Fear

"Abba, if it is so difficult to climb and so easy to be distracted, is it any wonder Luke spends so much time sitting beneath the shade of the cedar? It seems like such a tiring challenge for him."

"Gabriel, your observations are not wrong. The challenges are very real because the opposition to my purpose is highly determined, and Diablo's troops are well-trained."

"So how do your children face this fierce opposition?"

Abba turned slightly on his heel and tilting his head, beckoned with his eyes for Gabriel to look again at the shady place where Luke sat.

"See the shade, Gabriel?"

"Yes, what is it?"

"What do you notice? What do you see?"

"I see the vastness of the shade created by the branches, the strength of the limbs that give the shade and hold up so much snow in days of blizzards."

"And what else?"

"Ahh! Something interesting, but I am not sure what to make of it."

"Go on, Gabriel."

"Luke has taken his eyes off the valley, and he's looking up!"

"Is he alone?"

"Yes, Abba. No, Abba! Alone-ish. There are no people, but I am amazed at the number of birds in the tree. It seems Luke is amazed too. He is smiling."

As the two of them marveled at the sight of hundreds, maybe more, of birds nesting on the branches of the tree, God said, "On the mountain heights where I have planted it, it has produced branches and borne fruit and become a splendid cedar."

"Majestic, Abba."

"Birds of every kind can be found nesting. They find shelter in the shade of its branches." [Ezekiel 17:23]

"Good job, Abba, because there's no other tree in sight!"

"The sparrows nest there, Gabriel."

"Really?"

"Yes, look carefully. A sparrow is on every branch, yet not one will fall to the ground outside of my care." [Matthew 10:21-33]

"God?"

"What is it, Gabriel?"

"I often see them, sitting alone, but not under the cedar—in the valley, on the path, or just in a corner. They look forlorn, exhausted, beaten."

"They, Gabriel?"

"Your children, Luke, all of them at one time or another."

"All of them?"

"Well, most of them and quite often. It makes me sad to see them so dejected and despondent."

"Me too, Gabriel, me too." Abba exhaled slowly. "Do you know what makes them slump to the ground this way?"

"I suppose it is the circumstances. Or events? Or relationships? Or broken promises?"

"Yes, Gabriel, all that and more. But what is the reason that these things can keep their spirits down?"

"I don't know. I really don't know."

"Fear."

"Again, Abba? Fear again?"

Gabriel Understands the Task

"Fear of what this time, Abba?"

"Fear of being forgotten."

"Forgotten by whom?"

"They would say fear of being forgotten by those around them, fear of being considered insignificant, invalid, useless. Fear of amounting to little or nothing. Fear of not being loved."

"Yes, I see that. They are always seeking to be loved in the most bizarre ways."

"They cannot grasp that I have numbered the very hairs on their heads, and they are worth more than many sparrows." [Luke 12:7]

"They are loved by their Father, who gave them the shade of the magnificent cedar."

"And that's not all, Gabriel. Luke has chosen the sweetest of places to rest, protected by this great canopy of dark green needle-like leaves. He feels safe as he rests against the great trunk, and he watches as the birds demonstrate the great freedom they possess to live free under my watchful eye. They rise on the wind yet return to sing to me from the branches, knowing they can always dwell in the shelter of the Most High, resting in the shadow of the Almighty." [Psalm 91]

"Luke knows all this?"

"He is learning. Listen to his prayer:

> I will say of the Lord, 'He is my refuge
> and my fortress, my God in whom I trust.'
> Surely he will save me, cover me under His wings.
> His faithfulness will be my shield. [Psalm 91]

"There's hope in his voice, God. Hope!"

"No harm will overtake him, Gabriel."

"You commanded me, God, to guard him in all his ways."

"Yes, Gabriel, it is your job to lift him in your hands so that his foot will not strike against a stone on his climb." [Psalm 91:12]

→17←

Fast Growth

The young angel's mind was full of questions, his mind racing from thought to thought.

"When Luke is sitting beneath the cedar, I can relax a little, though, because you made it so that the serpent cannot get close to the cedar."

"I did tell you it's no ordinary tree. It grows like I want my children to grow. And when they choose to love and acknowledge me, I rescue them, protect them, deliver them, and honor them."

"How do you honor them?"

"With long life I will satisfy them."

"Satisfaction! I love that word, Abba. Will you tell me more about satisfaction?"

"Yes, but satisfaction is directly related to patience, so . . ."

"Okay, Abba, I'll wait."

A Rod for the Back of Fools

"Abba, Luke sat back down with a jolt."

"Yes, I saw him."

"What happened?"

"Love. To love is difficult, almost as difficult as being loved."

"You've lost me again, Abba."

"Luke saw one of his children in pain as he looked back down the valley."

"His children?"

"Yes, he is feeling what I feel, seeing what I see, and it is cutting deep. He lost the strength in his legs and the—"

"I can lift him in my hands!" Gabriel interjected, excited.

"Wait, Gabriel. Let him have this moment. He needs to know how I feel. I am showing him."

"What happened?"

"One of his sons has chosen to walk away from the mountain, and he can see him in the distance. He has lost sight of many of his sons who have chosen this same path."

"The father of lies?"

"Yes, yes . . . a whip for the horse, a bridle for the donkey—"

"And a rod for the back of fools!" finished Gabriel. [Proverbs 26:3]

"Gabriel, it is hard to watch your children suffer. And when the rod is of iron and the back is already bent, the father's suffering is great."

"Why is his back already bent?"

"Because this young man has never given me his burdens."

"He never came to you? Even though he was weary?" [Matthew 11:28]

"He came. Luke brought him to me. But he did not learn the lessons of the cedar."

"What do you mean? He didn't let you take his burdens? Didn't he know your burden is light?"

"Yes, he knew. He still knows. But I made them free to choose, Gabriel, and he decided to listen to the voice of his father."

Gabriel shook his head in disbelief "Let me guess, this father, I am so tired of him. Can't you put an end to this game, Abba?"

"I already have, Gabriel. I already have."

"So he must have whispered in that young man's ear again. Why do they listen, God?"

"Because they don't love me."

"What did Diablo promise him this time?"

"Fast growth, Gabriel. That's all, fast growth."

Climbing with Power!

"Abba, why do they always want to go so fast? Grow so quickly? So many times, I have seen Luke try to run and end up falling."

"Il ne faut pas avoir les yeux plus gros que le ventre!"

"Don't bite off more than you can chew? What do you mean, God?"

"I see your French has improved, Gabriel! You really want that island assignment, don't you?"

"I want to follow Luke's journey, Abba."

"Ahhh, then listen. He and the others want to grow fast because they think they know where they are going."

"So, they make plans?"

"Yes, in his heart a man plans his course."

"But you determine his steps!" [Proverbs 16:9]

"I want them to reach the top of the mountain, so I hold them to the path."

"When they let you, Abba."

"Yes, when they let me."

"What makes them let you plan their course?"

"Confidence, trust, patience, epignosis."

"Epi-what?"

"Eh-pig-know-sis, Gabriel. Precise, correct, intense knowing."

"Knowing what, Abba?"

"Knowing me."

"But they all know you, God. Even Diablo knows you, but he never lets you guide his steps."

"There are different kinds of knowing. When they climb alone, making their plans, dealing with success and failure as if it were their merit, they are not without knowledge . . ."

"But?"

"Many know me and even proclaim to others their pleasure of knowing who I am, trying to convince others in the valley to begin to climb as well. But when they share, those who listen can't help but look at the scars."

"What scars?"

"Look at Luke's legs and his heart. He has many marks and scars where he thought he knew the way and set off climbing without waiting for me."

"Like the disciples?"

"How do you mean, Gabriel?"

"You told them to stay in the city until you clothe them with power from the mountain." [Luke 24:49]

"It's true, Gabriel, you cannot climb without the power."

"If they know that, then why don't they wait?"

"Because of Other."

"Other?"

"Yes, they look at Other, and in their hearts they ask, 'What about him?' They fear that Other may beat them to the top."

"But it's not a race."

"No, it's an invitation to an encounter with me."

"Oh, yes. And what an encounter—the greatest wedding ceremony in history. On a mountain top!" [Revelation 21:9-10]

Gabriel's eyes lit up as he recalled the stories that God had revealed to him about the most fabled mountainous meeting of all time.

"And it doesn't matter when they arrive. I throw my arms around them all because they are all my sons and daughters. I love them all!"

Who's in Control?

"Epignosis, God?"

"What about it, Gabriel?"

"Luke is sitting, reflecting. Does he really know you?"

"Luke has always known me, with his mind. Even his spirit has been affected by my presence. He has been taught well."

"What do you mean?"

"My children have developed ways of thinking and teaching others according to their particular ideas."

"Huh?"

"They encourage those around them to think the same as they do, and much of what they teach is correct and good."

"But not all of it?"

"No, it's like this. When you look at the cedar, you see its magnificent symmetry and the shade created by its strong limbs, but do you remember where I planted it?"

"On the side of a mountain."

"Yes, unprotected from the elements and far from water."

"How does it survive?"

"Like Luke."

"I don't get it."

"Any tree can grow and produce fruit, right? The same can be said of man."

"How?"

"I gave them all gifts and talents that set them apart from one another, and with those talents they can achieve great success amongst their peers."

"Yes, I see them striving and working hard for success, so others will see them achieving, that's what they call it."

"True, but they have no control over the elements, Gabriel."

They both felt the early morning chill and folded their arms in unison across their chests. Gabriel looked at Abba as if to question, and God, raising his eyebrows, acknowledged, "Yes, son, that was me. Wind, sun, rain, snow, and chilly morning air. They do not control the ebb and flow of the tides or the dancing waters of the rivers, and they certainly have no power over each other."

"They like to think they do."

"Yes, but history shows them differently, Gabriel, doesn't it?"

"Yes, Abba, very differently."

Rooted and Grounded. Help Arrives!

"Luke!" said Gabriel.

"Luke? Yes, he has always been capable and has often had growth spurts, but until recently, he has been unaware of what it means to grow."

"Do you mind explaining that, Abba? What it means to grow?"

"Not at all. Let's start with the word *sagah*. It is easy, Gabriel, like summer flowers, to grow up and produce quickly; but it is not so easy to produce flowers, fruit, and fragrance that lasts.

"So sagah means what, Abba?"

"Threefold growth."

"Do you mean to grow up?"

"Yes, parents like to use that phrase even to criticize their children. As if growing up were the most important part or even the only part of growth."

Gabriel thought for a few minutes, and as God waited patiently, the young angel suggested another possibility. "What about growing down?"

"Yes, the cedar would bend and crack, breaking under the strain of the wind and weight of the snow, if it were not well-rooted in the ground."

"But the ground is so hard."

"Of course, that is why the cedar takes so long to reach maturity. It digs deep to be able to support the tribulation that it is called to endure."

"So, Luke grew up, and in his time of tribulation, he bent and broke?"

God leaned back, stretching his arms over his head. "Yes, one of his scars was made this way. When my children look at him in the valley and see where he broke, they see their scars and believe there to be no difference between him and them. They carry on along their paths, away from Luke, away from the mountain."

"But there are some would-be climbers who see Luke's scars and still want him to help them learn to climb the mountain, right?"

"Yes, because of prayer. People have always been praying for Luke, and those prayers have helped some roots to penetrate the rocky soil beneath. When the winds came, he bent and some boughs broke."

"But not all of them?"

"No, the trunk was rooted and grounded in love."

"So Luke was able to sense the breadth, length, depth, and height of your love? [Ephesians 3:17-18]

"Yes, so he would not be blown here and there by every wind." [Ephesians 4:14]

$\Rightarrow$19$\Leftarrow$

Valley Fears, Mountain Views

Gabriel sensed that the story of Luke's climb was not nearing the end, and he had a myriad of questions still to ask.

"Abba, if the cedar is slow-growing, and Luke is also slow in his climbing, how will Luke know that it is time to start his ascent again?"

"He already knows, but he is wisely waiting."

"For what?"

"Luke knows that there is fruit, lasting fruit, and he is desperate to experience it."

"You mean to taste it?"

"No, I mean to experience it! Luke is learning to trust me."

"Can you elaborate?"

"Many fruits can be tasted even before they are ready. Some people even like fruit that is hard and bitter. But I have called Luke and all of my family to experience the complete joy of the ripened fruit."

"How?"

"The cedar takes upwards of twenty years to produce its fruit, and when the fruits appear, they still need up to three more years to come to maturity. They are not edible. When the scaly, resinous cones open, however, they spread their pollen far and wide on the mountain winds.

"The pollen is accompanied by the fragrant aroma emanating from its dark brown bark and scented oil, thus spreading all the goodness from within the cedar far and wide to the delight of all within the reach of the winds. The cedar grows up, grows down, and grows out. The branches are home to many birds, and the pollen and aroma attract others to their qualities.

"It may bend, like Luke, when faced with trials of all kinds—but with joy in the face of trouble. And with patience, through perseverance, Luke's ascent becomes not only possible, but his faith is also strengthened. Many will see the deep love, mature and complete, that I have for him and be attracted to me through him as he grows down in his knowledge of me, up in his expressions of my love for him, and out as an expression of our love for all around us." [James 1:2-4]

A Glimpse of the Emerald Lake

"Abba, Luke is on his feet and seems pretty determined."

"Determined-angry or determined-peaceful?"

"Determined-peaceful, I think." In a low, sad tone, Gabriel continued, "That's another of your miracles, Abba, isn't it? Luke's peace at this moment."

"Yes, I suppose his peace goes beyond human understanding, given he has just heard that another of his sons has lost his way."

"What was it this time, Abba?"

"An overdose. A child of mine who suffered much until he chose on his own to walk away from my mountain, fists clenched and head bowed low . . . to his death." Sadness came over Abba, yet his words were light and unhurried: "Luke has just caught a glimpse of the Emerald Lake."

"What is that?"

"In Luke's mind, he thinks he has already seen absolute beauty—he calls it Emerald Lake. In the clear waters, he sees a reflection of who I am. I show him the reflection to remind him of all the wonderful things he is yet to see on the climb—all the things that one day he will see clearly when he meets me face-to-face and knows me fully.

"Luke knows he needs refreshment and a deeper vision of me to sustain him as he faces the challenges ahead, so he is ready to climb to new heights in pursuit of me. If he doesn't see me more clearly each day, the vision of his dying sons will take him back to the valley." [1 Corinthians 13:12]

⇢20⇠

The Overhang

Gabriel was unsure if he should speak because of what he saw lying ahead.

"Abba?"

"Yes?"

"Has Luke seen the overhang?"

"No, not yet, Gabriel. But he has already faced one projecting rock formation, and the next one is not his challenge but the challenge of those close behind. He will be their guide when they all arrive at the overhang together."

"You said he has already faced an overhang?"

"Yes, one of the most terrifying overhangs of all. In fact, overhangs like that have been appearing all over the mountain. Luke needed all the assistance he could get to help him get over his."

"But Abba, I don't remember Luke's overhang. And I certainly don't remember lots of people coming to his assistance at any point during the climb. Where was I?"

"You were further up the mountain, Gabriel. While he was struggling on the climb, a loose pile of rocks above threatened to fall on him. If you hadn't held them in place, we would have lost Luke forever. They would have hit him at his weakest point."

"So, that's why you had me all alone on that cliff face, for Luke."

"Yes, and my Son was by my side interceding for Luke all the time that you were on the cliff, and we thank you, Gabriel, just as Luke is thankful." [Romans 8:34]

"Please tell me more about the overhang."

"My children love to love and be loved, and they meet many challenges on the climb because of this."

"To love and be loved is a challenge?"

"Yes, ever since they took their eyes off me in the garden, they have been working the land, seeking approval and affirmation in all sorts of places."

"But they can still get their approval from you, can't they?"

"Of course. I am continually affirming them, but sometimes they come to a crossroads on their journey, where paths meet, and they need to take a stand."

"They need help from Wisdom?"

"Yes, but often they do not ask for Wisdom's help, even though I am always willing to send her regardless of the number of times they may need her guidance." [James 1:5]

"So, when I lost sight of Luke, he was at the overhang?"

"Yes, he was. The Climb Alones often see overhangs and spend time seeking ways to avoid them. Doubt creeps in and they forget that I am calling them and that I have promised never to leave them or forsake them." [Hebrews 13:5]

"Their ways are always in your full view, aren't they, God?"

"Yes, though they are afraid that the overhangs remove them from my view and thus from my help."

"How did Luke manage to defeat the overhang?"

"Luke began to climb late one evening. He had gained much knowledge, though he did lack in wisdom. He was climbing alone at that time, confident of his ability to scale the heights."

"I remember. Young and eager."

"Although he learned about hearing my voice, he was often persuaded to let his heart make covenants with other Climb Alones."

"Covenants are good, aren't they, Abba?"

"Yes, they can be, especially when they have me as the glue that binds the two climbers together. [Ecclesiastes 4:12]

"So, Luke made a covenant?"

"Yes, an agreement, an alliance, a name change—from Climb Alone to Climb Together to meet me at the summit."

"And what happened?"

"The climb was much more torturous than they had imagined, and Luke and his climbing partner both found that they did not have the strength to climb."

"What did they do?"

"They sought alternative routes and tried to go alone—together, but alone, on a pathway too difficult to walk without my help."

"Did they fall?"

"No, Gabriel. My law was in their hearts, and I would not let their feet slip." [Psalm 37:31]

"But did anyone help them?"

"Some other climbers tried to help, but they were unable to see the way ahead. The path behind became obscure, and they even had difficulty seeing what was right beside them. They were climbing while looking at their feet, unable to see the signposts or hear the words of warning."

"I see lots of your children trying to climb this way, Abba. Their heads are down, they're even holding hands, with gold bands on their fingers to identify their climbing partners."

"Yes, Gabriel, it was my idea—two of my children, male and female, climbing together, following my voice. It is wonderful to reach the top of the mountain together, and it makes the views along the way more amazing as they love to marvel together at my creation."

"But, God?"

"Yes?"

"I find lots of those gold bands discarded on the mountain. Seems they don't have much value."

"Oh, but they do, Gabriel. They have great value. Diablo has some tools, though, that easily remove bands from fingers and covenants from hearts."

Gabriel looked dismayed. "Could you explain?"

"Diablo stores most of his tools in the Shed of Modern Times behind Comparison's house. Pride and Selfishness have help from their friends to give the tools out to my children on the climb."

"Pride and Selfishness have friends?"

"Well, let's call them cousins. Lust, Envy, and Anger are always eager to help."

"I'm sure I have seen Lust on the mountain, Abba. From a distance, he looks a lot like Love."

"Yes, a master of disguise."

"Usually these minions wait until an overhang or a river that needs crossing before appearing with their tools."

"Like the River of Temptation?"

"Yes, and the Lake of Debt where the Rope Bridge of Insecurity is enough to scare even experienced climbers."

"Envy usually approaches at the Valley of Greener Grass, on the other side of the fence separating Comparison's house from his neighbors, the Betters."

"I've seen that, Abba. Lust and Anger often wait for the Ravine of Abuse where memory alone blinds the climbers, leaving them unaware of who is handing them the tools."

"Exactly, and the old adversary Rejection, under the pretense of protection, is often the one who nudges them so that they fall into the ravine."

"Where are Trust and Discernment at times like this?"

"Easily forgotten, unfortunately."

"That's not surprising, God, because you would never see Trust and Discernment on the mountain without Patience and Perseverance."

"And that is why they take off their gold bands. They are told that the gold bands will prevent them from holding the tools properly. Diablo's helpers remind them that it is easier to climb alone."

"But that's not true."

"No, Gabriel, never true."

"But once they have taken off the bands, what happens?"

"They call it freedom when really it is an elaborate trap, a shortcut that exalts pleasure and takes them further away from the path, further from the top of the mountain, and further from me."

"If they take off the gold band, can they never reach the top of the mountain?"

"Yes, they can, but the pathway is much steeper."

→21←

The Toughest of Choices

"Did Luke take off his gold band, Abba?"

"Not exactly. He and his climbing partner were beginning the ascent when they reached a challenging part of the climb, made even more difficult because she didn't have the strength to go on."

"What did they do?"

"Luke was accustomed to relying on gifts and talents—and remember that he has always struggled with Patience—so he insisted on continuing the climb. But she was not able. One night, with the wind howling and the cold biting, Luke pushed on to try and find a sheltered spot to rest."

"What happened next?"

"When the sun came up in the morning, he saw where he was, alone, upside down, under an overhang. He was clinging on for dear life."

"Where was his partner?"

"She had decided not to attempt this part of the climb and had taken a different path. Since it was dark, Luke did not see her go."

"Did they meet up again?"

"No, sadly, and Luke held on to that overhang until the gold band cut into his finger, and blood began to flow. Finally, he lifted his eyes to me and cried out to me. He took off the gold band to stop the pain, though I did not tell him to do so.

"I could have healed his hand and his heart, but he chose to ask me to strengthen his feeble arms and weak knees and make level paths for his feet. [Hebrews 12:12-15] That was when I commanded you to lift him up." [Psalm 91:11-12]

"And what about his climbing partner?"

Without looking at Gabriel, Abba shifted his gaze to the horizon. "That is a conversation for another angel."

⇢22⇠

Father, Can I Forgive?

"Windows."

"Sorry, God, what was that? Did you say 'windows'?"

"Yes, windows. They are used to see what is happening without necessarily involving oneself."

"Abba? Is there a point to this talk of windows?"

"I like to use them to teach my children about love."

"How?"

"I show them things, people, places, events . . . look." God pointed at a climber on his journey.

"Who is that? I can see him clearly through this window."

"That is Raul Alone, precious Raul."

"Why is he all alone?"

"Actually, he is not. It's just that you are only able to see him. Those around him are invisible to you."

"He looks so sad."

"Yes, he does . . . But this image you see is not from today. It is an old image that I wanted to show you."

As God spoke once again, tears rolled gently down his cheek and dropped onto his arms that were folded across his chest.

Gabriel, moved in his spirit, felt a knot in his throat, and the warmth of a tear slide down his face.

"Raul is coming to terms with losing his father. He is fourteen in this image and has been grieving for some time."

"Did his father recently die?"

"No, his dad is still there."

"I don't understand."

"Raul's father was away on a business trip when his son was born, he was drinking with his friends when his uncle abused Raul, and he was away at a climber's conference when Raul broke his arm. When Raul's girlfriend got pregnant and lost the baby, his father was too tired and angry to listen and give wise counsel to his son about the climb ahead."

"And now?"

"Raul misses his dad, and the pain is indescribable. In fact, it is so difficult to describe the pain that comes when the father is not present that an entire generation has chosen to ignore the effects of this wound."

"Abba? Did I see right? Raul's father took off his gold band and quickly replaced it with another? Belonging to someone else?"

"Yes, and Raul wears the scars, which he easily could have avoided if his father had stopped long enough to listen and to love."

"So many of your children have no father, Abba."

"Yes, Gabriel, and this, I must say, is one of the greatest reasons why the climb is so difficult, why so many climb alone, and why so many more run away."

"Many of them don't even know who their father is."

"That is why I gave other climbers gifts specifically for this situation. They are a small group that I call the Fosters. I send my angels with them to tend to climbers who are hurt."

"Which angels do you send? Do I know them?"

"You see them often, Gabriel. They are all over the mountain and often in the valley too—Empathy, Grace, Patience, Compassion, and Mercy. A wonderful team. Not the most organized but really good friends of my Son, Emanuel."

"I love to spend time with that group, but it is hard to talk much with them because they are always busy. And another thing, why do they all carry a small flask in their belts?"

"The balm of forgiveness. Without it, they could not help Raul and the others find me on the mountain. It is forgiveness that soothes the pain and makes it possible to love again, to trust again. Many make the mistake of refusing the balm of forgiveness. Still they discover that the sores of regret and resentment, which develop where bad memories have left indelible marks, are impossible to remove without forgiveness."

"There is so much sadness, Abba. My heart breaks. I can only imagine how you feel to see your children experience so much that you didn't design for them."

"Yes, Gabriel. And the list is not short: sexual immorality, impurity, debauchery, idolatry, witchcraft, hatred, discord, jealousy, fits of rage, selfish ambition, dissensions, factions, envy, drunkenness, and orgies." [Galatians 5]

"But all that filth is only in the valley. You wouldn't find those things on the mountain, surely."

"You would be surprised, Gabriel, at what they try to take up the mountain with them."

Good Fruit on the Climb

"Is there redemption, Abba? Or, if all that is happening, is all lost?"

"Gabriel, it is never lost, and if only one of my children is hurting and in need, I will leave the rest and go and rescue that one. And I have faithful children, Gabriel, who serve me and seek out the broken, the marginalized, and the downtrodden.

"They are faithful children who seek to know me and make me known in the valleys and on the mountains. I give excellent fruit to those that seek me with all their heart. [Luke 15:4; Jeremiah 29:14]

"Fruit, Abba? Tell me more. I feel the need to have my spirit lifted."

"Beautiful trees are on the mountain, laden with so much good fruit: love, joy, peace, patience, kindness, goodness, faithfulness, and self-control."

"The fruit is for those who keep in step with your spirit on the climb, isn't it, God? Not for those who take shortcuts." [Galatians 5:22-25]

→ 23 ←

Grace and Beauty

"God, I've been accompanying Luke's climb now for a long time. I understand that you don't need me to hold his hand. I can see that he can hear your voice and make good decisions to avoid the caves of greed and the slippery slopes of the glacier of ignorance. Pride has taken it upon himself to invite Luke to the Village of Aye continually, but Luke has never stayed the night, even though he has had a drink or two at the Pub-on-the-Pond-of-Self."

"You have been observant, Gabriel. Do you have a point?"

"Yes, Abba, I do. I have a question. I always thought that Grace and Beauty are two separate people. But they're not, are they?"

Without waiting for an answer, Gabriel continued, "I see Luke on that high, narrow path, the one that skirts the mountain at its most dangerous point, just before the Peak of New Hope. I know he's exhausted and afraid. He doesn't like heights, does he?"

"The views from there are spectacular, Gabriel. To his left, the majestic mountains rise into the clouds, and to the right, the ravine where my raging, life-giving waters tumble down to the valley. The rain pouring down stings as it hits the climbers, and the stone path continually moving beneath Luke's feet creates a sense of insecurity. Falling is what Luke fears most."

"Yes, God, I can see . . . and feel his fear. It's tangible."

"But you asked me about Grace-and-Beauty?"

"She's been on the mountain for some time, hasn't she?"

"Yes, I had to hold her very tight in the beginning. She met Hope-in-Dark-Places at the foot of the mountain and has held on to Hope ever since, never letting go. Very determined that child of mine."

"Abba, she faced fear early in the climb, didn't she?"

"Yes, she did, Gabriel. Its spirit still returns to haunt her at times, but she never was tempted into Comparison's House, so old Self-Pity never had a chance to influence her.

"But for quite some time she has been shadowing Luke, climbing with him. Why is that?"

God smiled. "Gabriel, Grace-and-Beauty is my gift to Luke. She is firm and steadfast, constant and wise—a descendant of the family of Deep-Roots, looking forward and not backward. Luke is often the opposite."

"And it was your idea that they climb together?"

"No, it was their choice."

"Looks like a pretty good decision.

God felt pity as he recalled Luke's anguish with the lists and tables on the day he had met Grace-and-Beauty on the mountain.

"All my children need to build on good foundations, and they all need to calculate the cost before beginning to climb the mountain. But counting the cost and building on good foundations is not enough." [Luke14:28-30]

"Not enough? Please explain."

"Because when I shake the foundations, pillars must be in place for me to hold firm. Otherwise, all that is will cease to be. My plan has always been to sit my children with me, like special treasures by my side in my kingdom. But to achieve my plan, there must be pillars." [Psalm 75:3, Malachi 3:1, Ephesians 2:6, Zechariah 9:16]

"What kind of pillars?"

"To be able to build my kingdom, Gabriel, I need to have pillars in place for all that I wish to construct. My children need to set down their roots and grow, like strong cedars, in my garden. Others are like corner pillars; I test them by shaking the foundations. Those that remain standing I use to build my Kingdom." [Psalm 144:12; Job 9:6]

"You are building a kingdom with Peter and Grace-and-Beauty?"

"Yes, Gabriel, the City of Strong-Family, just a few miles from the fastest growing city in Diablo's kingdom."

Gabriel had seen many people coming and going from Diablo's most popular city, though he noticed that more people were coming than going.

"Are you talking about Modern Society?"

"Yes, Gabriel. Mayor Forward Thinking has been in deep conversation with the philosophers David Septian, Damon Seeved, and Emanuel Pulate."

"Even Mani is involved, Abba? How sad."

"They have written creeds, regulations, and even established new versions of right and wrong."

"I know God, and I am amazed at the number of people whose inquisitiveness leads them to the city."

"Not their inquisitiveness, Gabriel. Their hearts are bent on doing the will of their father, Diablo. They are his children, after all."

→24←

Equipped To Climb

"Abba, am I right in thinking that the equipment needed to climb the mountain can only be purchased in the City of Strong-Family?"

"Not exactly, but it is certainly the best way to begin the climb. The equipment doesn't need to be purchased, though. It is free for all my children." [Ephesians 2:8-9]

"Yes, I've seen some who have tried to climb the mountain with the equipment they have bought themselves—Self-Help equipment. They spend much time boasting about the quality of their ropes and climbing boots."

"Not surprising, really, Gabriel. Do you know the owner of the Self-Help Climbing Retail Store?

"No, who is it?"

"None other than our wily friend, Comparison."

"Unbelievable. It's no wonder they have such a hard time finding the right path. Traps are everywhere."

"And they are always looking for the loudest, strongest, biggest, greatest, and most colorful of everything, Gabriel."

"Yet you choose the weak and foolish things to shame the strong and wise." [1 Corinthians 1:27]

"I am a jealous God. I won't share my glory with another." [Exodus 34:14; Isaiah 42:8]

Two Sets of Equipment

"You said it isn't absolutely necessary to get the equipment from the City of Strong-Family?"

"No, there is another way."

"What is it?"

"There must always be somebody from Strong-Family to receive the equipment, but usually I give my children two sets of everything. One for themselves and one to give away to someone they meet on their journey."

"What a great idea, Abba. That's when we really see if they love one another."

"Some of them, however, only take one set with them and join the throngs of Climb Alones. Then when they meet others on the road to the mountain, they avoid eye contact because they know they have left behind the very thing they need to help the other climb."

"How sad. You mean many more could climb the mountain if only your children would be more courageous and willing to serve others?"

"Something like that, Gabriel, something like that."

Building a Strong Family

"Are Luke and Grace-and-Beauty building a strong family, Abba?"

"They are certainly paying attention to my voice on the subject, and they are considering how many others they can encourage to carry more equipment with them on the climb, to rescue fallen climbers and help others whose equipment has broken."

"Would Luke be able to do that on his own?"

"No, he needs the constant encouragement of Grace and the vision of Beauty to be able to climb. The gold band he has put on his finger reminds him of all my promises. I will never leave them or forsake them on their climb." [Deuteronomy 31:8]

The Shade of a Juniper Tree

"So, Abba, Luke has been climbing for some time. Let me see if I can get this all straight in my mind."

"Okay. Go on, Gabriel."

"You long to meet with Luke at the summit, so you call him to the mountain."

"Yes, that's the beginning."

"But it's harder for Luke if you call him first, right? I don't remember if you ever explained that to me."

God was enjoying the young angel's inquisitiveness and wanted to make this point very clear, so they sat down under the shade of a juniper tree, and he took Gabriel through the rudimentary basics of a call.

"Gabriel, you know how much I love my children, don't you?"

"Yes, Abba, so much that you gave your only Son to die for them so that they could be with you forever on the mountaintop." [John 3:16]

"I love them and I know them," Abba said, smiling. "I knitted them together in their mother's womb and set them in families for their mutual benefit. The love that a family is capable of showing mirrors my love." [Psalm 139:13]

"Does it really, God? Are you sure? As I watch them with their families, I rarely see them loving each other. I usually see them covering up the truth, raising their voices, and pretending to be something they are not. It's anything but love and certainly not like your love."

"How would you describe my love then, Gabriel? What do you hope to see in their families if their love is to look like mine?"

Gabriel, thoughtful but confident, replied quickly, "You always tell me that love is kind and patient."

"Yes, though sometimes it is one person's kindness that teaches patience to the other."

"And you say that love is not proud and does not boast. That's difficult for them when they have success, Abba, especially the young boys."

"Not just the young boys, Gabriel, the men. They all struggle with this. If there is someone in the family, someone who does not struggle with envy and has managed to avoid Comparison's house, then this person's example teaches the rest how to honor others and how to seek the best for those around them. When a person models a spirit of grateful generosity, they will find it tough to soak in boastful pride."

Gabriel quickly said, "Seems like the mothers are often good at that bit, Abba."

"Yes, that is often the case."

"The love you have taught me doesn't focus on what went wrong, does it? Perfect love, the way you describe it, drives out all fear and keeps anger at bay."

"Fear is the motivation behind so much anger, but true love rejoices in the truth, not in evil, so it helps reduce anger."

"Where true love exists, they always seem better protected, more trusting, and full of hope. Is that really true, Abba?"

"The men are good at protecting the ones they love when they truly love those around them and not just themselves."

"But it seems so hard for their families to stay together. Why is that, when their families are supposed to be built on love?"

"True love always perseveres, Gabriel, even through hard times. True love never fails." [1 Corinthians 13:8]

"And for the love of a family to never fail, everyone needs to do their part, don't they?"

"Yes, everyone. But the responsibility is with the father. He must seek me first and must love and honor his wife. Then, and only then, can he expect that his children will follow his instructions. He must start his children off on the way they should go, and if he has learned to love his family as I love my children, then his sons and daughters will not turn from his teachings as they get older." [1 Corinthians 13; Proverbs 22:6]

⇒26⇐

The Clearing

"I set Luke in his family, and I set about instructing his father, William. And through William, I sowed seeds, taught principles, established my values, laid foundations, and set pillars in place."

"Then why has it been such a challenge for Luke to understand the simplicity of your words? Why has he deviated so frequently from your path?"

"Why do you ask so specifically about Luke? This question you can ask about all my children. And the answer is simple, yet eternal."

"Please explain, God. Sometimes I don't follow your train of thought."

"Gabriel, can you see where Luke is at this very moment on the mountain?"

He looked, squinting through the early evening sun until his eyes rested on Luke as he arrived at a clearing.

"That's not an ordinary clearing, is it?"

"No, most of the Climb Alones avoid this type of clearing. It's not the easiest place to visit."

"Why would they avoid a clearing, God?"

"For the same reason that they enjoy the results of the olive press but are rarely interested in the process through which the olive passes."

"Gethsemane,[1] Abba! I have watched the workers in the field beating the olive trees for the ripe olives to fall to the ground, then the olives being crushed in the press and the blood-red hue of the life-giving pulp being squeezed from the fruit to release the oil. That oil so delicious and healthy. Good for the heart.

"Did you ever think about that, Abba? The beating of the olive tree and the crushing of the olive, the smearing of the paste onto burlap mats, bleeding it of its inherent goodness. Messiah![2] [Luke 23:34] Even the useless parts of the pulp-like paste are useful for making soap. Crushing a simple olive, washing clean the hands, and purifying the heart of those that want to climb your mountain, Abba, is pretty fascinating." [Psalm 24:4]

"Why is that interesting to you, Gabriel?"

"It seems incredible to me that something so insignificant as an olive could produce so much goodness. And that from your mountains, from your Son's birthplace, would come life-giving oil bringing health and healing to all nations.

The Threshing Floor

"And the clearing God? Is there an olive press in the clearing?"

"No, Gabriel, not in this clearing."

"What is so special about this clearing on the climb? Why do the Climb Alones avoid it?"

"Remember that I said to you that Luke was looking at his hands and considering them unclean, and reflecting on his heart and finding himself impure?"

"Yeah, he considered himself unfit to climb your mountain."

"One of the reasons is because he chose the Path of Least Resistance in an early part of the climb. Instead of letting me help them by searching their hearts and examining their minds, they avoid me and hide from me."

"As if that were possible, Abba." [Jeremiah 17:10; 23:24] They avoid the clearing and go where?"

"Other paths are often tempting, but avoiding the clearing almost always has the same result."

"What result?"

"Remember that they are trying to climb a mountain to meet with me. There are a lot of pitfalls, high ledges, and wrong turns on the ascent."

"The clearing?"

"It is one of the places where they can check their equipment, evaluate their climbing strategies, and look at the map. They must make sure they make any necessary adjustments to avoid the risks that lie ahead."

"And if they don't?"

"Their paths become slippery and lead to darkness. It is almost certain they will fall and have to start the climb again." [Jeremiah 23:12]

"Oh, no. That's terrible. All because they won't stop in the clearing?"

"Yes, the clearing is known as the Threshing Floor. King David knew the value of the threshing floor only too well." [2 Samuel 24:24-25]

Removing the Burdens That Remain

"But what happens there, Abba? At the Threshing Floor?"

"The wheat is separated from the chaff."

"What do you mean? Do the climbers have to take the wheat with them on the climb?"

"No, but like the wheat, the climbers must present all that they are to me when they get to the clearing."

"All that they are?"

"Yes, Gabriel. All that they are. They cannot complete the

climb to meet me at the summit if they insist on carrying with them things that will hold them back, weigh them down, blur their vision, or trip them up."

"And you say Luke is there right now, on the threshing floor?"

"Yes, he has chosen to rest there. He knows that this is the last clearing before the summit, and he is determined to lighten his load by letting me remove what remains of his burdens."

"Can you tell me which burdens he still carries, Abba?"

"Of course. You are, after all, the responsible angel in this case."

----

[1] Gethsemane: The name of an olive-yard at the foot of the Mount of Olives, to which Jesus was wont to retire (Luke 22:39) with his disciples, and which is especially memorable as being the scene of his agony (Mark 14:32 ; John 18:1 ; Luke 22:44).

[2] Messiah:The term "messiah" is the translation of the Hebrew term masiah [jyiv'm], which is derived from the verb masah, meaning to smear or anoint
https://www.biblestudytools.com/dictionary/messiah/

⇢27⇠

Pride Comes Before a Fall

Gabriel, intrigued, noticed that Luke had sat down on one side of the threshing floor but that Grace-and-Beauty had moved silently to another part of the clearing.

God saw that Gabriel was readying himself to ask a question, but before the words could leave his mouth, Abba said, "Luke and Grace-and-Beauty have been climbing together for some time now, holding on to each other. Sometimes desperately, sometimes lovingly, sometimes only because they know that they should honor the covenant. But when they arrived at the clearing, they both understood the importance of this time.

"I will uphold them on the next stage of their journey, if they delight in me, let go of their objectives, and embrace my dreams for them. If they trust me and wait on me, I will give them the desires of their heart. They may stumble, but they will not fall. [Psalm 37]

"What would stop them from trusting completely in you?"

"The ten commandments, Gabriel. They want me to carry them to their destiny like a father carries his son in the wilderness, but I am not able to carry them unless they turn their back on the evil one and devote their hearts completely to me." [Deuteronomy 1:31; 2 Kings 16:9]

"The ten commandments, God? Really? They are still struggling with the basics?"

"Yes, the Climb Alones believe that once they have said 'I do' to me, they can choose only a few of my laws, and I will turn a blind eye to the rest."

"And the threshing floor is where you address this quandary?"

"Yes, for those humble enough to stop, to wait, and to look longingly to me for help."

Chaff, Wind, and Fire

"Why is the threshing floor in a clearing, Abba?"

"Because I need the wind to help with the separation process. And then the fire burns up the rubbish, which they are leaving behind."

"Ah, I see God . . . they need to separate themselves for this time. The walls of the city are too high and the buildings too close. The wind would not be able to do its work. The winnowing fork would work in vain." [Luke 3:17]

"The walls of the city, and the walls of their hearts, Gabriel, are all too closed in, too high, preventing me from doing what I do best—bringing forth good fruit from the vine. If they remain in the city, the unquenchable fire cannot be released to burn away the chaff. But if they come humbly to the threshing floor, and remain in me, together we can do anything." [John 15:5]

"Do they come freely to the clearing, Abba?"

"Yes, I will not force them."

"The threshing process, is it easy? Is it quick? Can Luke continue his climb soon?"

"There is no time frame for purification. Like silver and gold in the furnace, if once is not enough, they must return again and again to burn away all that is impure. It's the furnace of affliction. [Isaiah 48:10]

Gabriel slid down to the ground, his legs folding under him as he thought of Luke submitting himself to hardship by choice to complete the journey to the top of the mountain.

"The affliction you speak of, God, why can't it be a simpler, gentler process?"

"Gabriel, my children must die to their sin. As the wheat cannot remain inside the kernel, so my children cannot remain alive within their sin. If they choose to climb on, carrying with them their backpack full of lies and deceit, pride, greed, self-pity, and sexual impurity, the required equipment needed for climbing to the summit will not fit them. They will be unable to ascend further.

"Many do try to carry on, but as Climb Alones, they return to their circular routes, hiding their true nature, pretending to know the way but never admitting their need for help and never arriving in my presence.

"Not only that, but those who choose to hide their weaknesses are always ready to offer advice to other climbers who arrive at the clearing, convincing many to struggle on with their heavy weights still attached. They don't realize that all they need to do is to give me their burdens so I can release them to climb the final ascent in the rarefied air where their full backpacks make the climb impossible." [Matthew 11:28-30]

"So, as the wheat is only useful once it is separated from the glumes, lemmas, and paleae, so your children will only be free to love and serve you fully once they have broken away from those things that hold them."

"That's right, Gabriel. To break away, they must have a willing heart—willing to surrender, willing to do whatever it takes . . ."

"How do they break away? How can Luke be free from the things that have slowed him down on the climb?"

"The tribula, Gabriel.[1] As the farmer attaches the tribula to the mule and watches as it crushes the grain, so too my spirit using his tribula tends to my children who willingly arrive at the threshing floor."

"Don't Diablo and his henchmen try to stop the process?"

"Oh, yes, they do. It is one of the most bizarre battles to watch unfold. Diablo and his minions, Bruise, Beat, and Behead believe that they are driving the last nails in the coffin of hope for my children, as if their attacks at the threshing floor will finally convince my children to turn their backs on me."

"And they don't? They don't turn their backs on you?"

"No, Gabriel. Exactly the opposite. Those who willingly submit themselves to the threshing floor understand that I, and only I, allow trial, affliction, tribulation, and persecution in this clearing. And they approach these trials with joy. It takes Diablo to the breaking point of desperation. What he means for harm I use to perfect my work."

"To leave your children pure and useful in your hand. Ready for any good work." [James 1:2-4; 2 Timothy 2:21]

"Yes, Gabriel. Yes."

----

[1] *trībulum (trīvol-), i, n. tero, a threshing-sledge, consisting of a wooden platform studded underneath with sharp pieces of flint or with iron teeth http://latinlexicon.org/definition.php?p1=2060610

⇒28⇐

Weapons for War

Down in the valley below, many were considering the ascent. The rules in the valley, it seemed, were changing. But the mountain remained the same. People wandered to and fro, some enjoying the late afternoon shadows cast by the mountain, whose imposing beauty rested beneath the twilight sky. Others pretended the mountain did not exist.

The pathways to begin the ascent were becoming more and more difficult to find. Weary travelers, having wandered for days on end in the valleys to locate the most convenient starting point for their climb, were left confused and exhausted. They often chose to sit alone at the foot of the mountain, head bowed and heart dejected at the thought of being confined to the valley forever.

Gabriel pondered this scene and recalled Luke's beginnings.

He thought about those shepherds whose words, wise in their own minds, had once upon a time led Luke to the church at Shady Corners, where he would learn the tricks of Diablo entrenched in hollow liturgy.

He marveled as he remembered Abba stooping to look for Luke, lifting him from the dust cloud, which had long since settled over Modern Society. [Psalm 113:6-7]

Gabriel knew that God was the one who graciously and compassionately protected Luke's simple heart, delivering his eyes from tears and his feet from stumbling so that they could walk together joyfully on the heights. [Psalm 116:6,8; Isaiah 58:14]

Gabriel was all too aware of the many good folks whom Luke had encountered in the valley before he had begun his climb. Some had been to the mountaintop and had been willing to return to the valley to serve Abba by reaching out to Others.

This, Gabriel knew, was always a risk for climbers who had been to the summit and met God face-to-face. For they would need to renounce all and return from where they had come, not knowing if they would be able to climb a second time but assured that the joy of having met with Abba would be their strength. For after enjoying all the goodness of his presence, they were given a chance to return to be a blessing for those who were unprepared in the valley below. [Luke 14; Nehemiah 8:10]

There in the valley, Luke had been given clues as to where to begin and instructions on how to avoid the lure of the town of Bright Lights, which drew so many of his companions away from the mountain.

And he had been given the Word, which at first he had not understood. However, it had become his greatest treasure on the ascent, revealing Abba's secrets, guiding his steps, and aiding him in guarding his heart against the attacks of Diablo's followers, many of whom disguised themselves as climbers looking just like Luke. [Proverbs 4:23]

For a time, Abba sat and watched as Gabriel remembered in silence. But he wanted to draw Gabriel's attention to one more thing.

Crossing the Bridge of Self

"Gabriel, have you notice how difficult it is for my children to take each step on the mountain confidently?"

"Yeah, their slow pace is excruciating for me to watch."

"But do you have a theory as to why they are so slow?"

"You have already told me that they must follow your voice, so I assume the difficult time they have in hearing you must be the reason."

"Yes, that is the most fundamental issue. But there is a second, very damaging condition that is embraced in the valley as a life principle and carried up the mountain by almost all of my children until they cross the Bridge of Self-Acceptance, which is the only way over the River of Identity.

"Did Luke already cross that bridge?"

"Yes, but as with many others, sometimes he returns to drink from the water in the river and is once again surprised at the reflection he sees as he drinks. His identity, you see, is firmly rooted in me, in my family. But the water in the River of Identity flows straight from the Fount of Fear and not from my temple."

"The Fount of Fear? Then he must cry out for your perfect love to defeat this identity crisis."

"No, Gabriel, not this time. For the river that flows from the Fount of Fear flows through the town of Man, and the fear of man is a condition that can only be addressed by those who have more fear of me than they have of their fellow man."

"Fear of you, Lord?"

"Yes. When they fear each other's opinions, they slide into the Pit of Untruth, where they meet young White Lie, an apparently harmless climber who encourages them to demonstrate their worth to each other by improving their image, qualifications, and possessions. It becomes hard for them to be honest with each other as they want to avoid making enemies at all costs.

"Afraid of the reactions of their friends, my children act and react to please others, disregarding truth and playing instead into the hands of Diablo, who loves to see them cowering behind his well-trained coaches False Humility and Criticism.

"But I did not give them a spirit of timidity but of power, love, and self-discipline so they may take a stand with truth and know that I will always be with them and never forsake them on the climb." [2 Timothy 1:7]

"They really can rise against the wicked and stand against evil?"

"Gabriel, my unfailing love, my help, is always available. The climb may be steep, the challenges great, and their faith as small as a mustard seed, but I have promised that I will not let the feet slip of those who fear me." [Psalm 94:16-18]

⇢29⇠

Tears of Joy

Abba's eyes surveyed the whole mountain, and seeing those whose hearts were fully devoted to him moved him to tears of joy. He instructed his angels and his spirit to strengthen those who continued to look to the mountain for their help while climbing. [2 Chronicles 16:9] Finally, he turned to the young angel.

"Gabriel, how is Luke?" he asked in a hushed tone.

Gabriel swung around on his heel and scanned the mountain, seeing Luke beginning his final ascent.

"Luke looks well, Abba. Strong and encouraged. Your grace has reached his heart, and he is marveling at the beauty of the view in all directions."

"Is he alone?"

"Yes. Why is that? Shouldn't he at least be with Grace-and-Beauty? Has he returned to being a Climb Alone?" Gabriel was shocked at the thought.

"Gabriel, the final ascent is always completed alone. Grace-and-Beauty has already arrived, and Luke is not far behind."

Gabriel noticed many small groups of climbers sitting together with hands raised and heads bowed. These small groups were dotted all over the mountain, and it seemed to the young angel, that there were more of these small groups than in bygone days.

Their climbing strategy, so it seemed, consisted of singing and proclaiming words to declare the nature of the faithful God who was calling them up the mountain. Sitting with them in their small groups were some of the angels sent to help those climbers who recognized their need for assistance.

There was Michael, always on the lookout to protect the climbers from attacks from Lucifer and Apollyon. The singers Gratitude, Thanksgiving, and Joyful-Always were with Michael. Grace-and-Beauty often sat in these groups and seemed to find great strength for her climb while singing.

Even Luke had discovered that when he was with these folks, he was able to understand more clearly the path he was required to follow.

"Abba, where are Niel and Isa? Shouldn't they be with their parents?"

"They are with them, Gabriel, but Luke and Grace-and-Beauty have understood that for this part of the climb, they need to release their children into my hands. Don't worry. I am assigning angels to accompany these two young climbers. They too will reach the summit and meet with me at the appointed time.

"Today the children are just initiating their ascent and are in the City of Strong-Family, getting measured for their climbing equipment."

"Is that Apollyon waiting for them on the path outside the city?"

Gabriel appeared nervous at the thought of Apollyon waiting for the children, but God was quick to see the anxiety and eased Gabriel's concerns.

"Gabriel, your dear friend Michael is at the city gate with a sword drawn. Apollyon has obviously not remembered the whole story."

"I am, and I have spoken," Abba said with a broad grin across his face. [Isaiah 49:22-26]

⇒30⇐

Who Am I?

The mountain has been the focus of the battle since the days of Moses and the children of Israel. God had always made it clear that one should approach the mountain with great trepidation and humility. At the same time, God's enemy, Diablo, does all within his power to not only prevent God's children from climbing but also from even recognizing the existence of the mountain.

Gabriel was amazed as he contemplated Luke's complicated, drawn-out ascent. He recalled the tears, the stubborn heart, and the critical spirit that had accompanied Luke for most of the climb. He also reflected on the strong winds that had threatened to blow Luke off course at various points along the path.

With his head slightly tilted to one side and a look of resolve in his eyes, Gabriel asked his most serious question to date. "God, how can they make it? Your children. To meet with you on top of the mountain? The challenge is so great, the winds so strong, and the opposition so furiously determined. It seems an impossible challenge, Abba."

God's reply was unexpected, but Gabriel felt his heart well up inside him as he listened.

"Gabriel, why do you sometimes call me God and at other times Abba?"

"I didn't realize I did that."

"But there is a reason, and it is the key to the ascent and the encounter."

As if it were a great orchestra, one-by-one, the noises of the mountain receded.

Silence descended slowly on the scene, and a wonderful peace rolled in like sea mist.

"Abba Father!" Gabriel exclaimed.

Tears rolled uncontrollably down his face, and he fell, prostrate before the Almighty God, his heart torn wide open. From his mouth poured these words: "Worthy is the Lamb who was slaughtered—to receive power and riches, wisdom and strength, and honor and glory and blessing. Blessing and honor and glory and power belong to the one sitting on the throne and to the Lamb forever and ever." [Revelation 5:13]

At that moment, millions of angels joined in the song of Gabriel's heart, and the mountain was awash with joy and the glory of God.

God was no longer standing but was seated on a throne and had the appearance of a lamb. Gathered around the throne were climbers from a myriad of tribes, languages, peoples, and nations.

Gabriel caught a glimpse of the victory, which he knew would come when this scene would be complete.

Gabriel saw God as he truly is—all-powerful with authority over all created and uncreated things. At that moment, he saw God's heart, which revealed the deep love of a father whose patience and love know no end, whose joy at receiving his children at the top of the mountain is as complete as it is profound. These were children adopted into the family of the God of the mountain.

"Abba Father!" proclaimed Gabriel.

"Abba Father!" proclaimed Luke. [Revelation 5:9,11-13]

⇢31⇠

The Summit

"Abba, what did you say to Luke when you met him at the top of the mountain?"

"I said the same things I have always said, Gabriel. I have never lied to Luke, nor hidden anything from him. I am not a man." [Numbers 23:19]

"I know, God, but what about Luke? There were so many times when he didn't listen to you, when he couldn't hear you, when he let the sounds of the valley drown out your voice."

"When he chose to ignore me?"

"Exactly."

"Gabriel, I know the plans I have for Luke, plans to prosper him and not to harm him, to give him a hope and a future. He will call on me and I will answer him. He has been seeking me with all his heart and has found me." [Jeremiah 29:11-13]

"So, he has arrived at the end of his journey?"

"No, Gabriel. Luke has arrived at the top of the mountain. This, dear Gabriel, is the start of another great climb."

Afterword

David to Solomon; Isaac to Jacob; Billy to Franklin... William to Luke...Fathers to sons (and daughters), give careful thought to your ways:

Proverbs 4

1 Listen, my sons, to a father's instruction; pay attention and gain understanding.

2 I give you sound learning, so do not forsake my teaching.

3 For I too was a son to my father, still tender, and cherished by my mother.

4 Then he taught me, and he said to me, 'Take hold of my words with all your heart; keep my commands, and you will live.

5 Get wisdom, get understanding; do not forget my words or turn away from them.

6 Do not forsake wisdom, and she will protect you; love her, and she will watch over you.

7 The beginning of wisdom is this: Get wisdom. Though it cost all you have, get understanding.

8 Cherish her, and she will exalt you; embrace her, and she will honor you.

9 She will give you a garland to grace your head and present you with a glorious crown.'

10 Listen, my son, accept what I say, and the years of your life will be many.

11 I instruct you in the way of wisdom and lead you along straight paths.

12 When you walk, your steps will not be hampered; when you run, you will not stumble.

13 Hold on to instruction, do not let it go; guard it well, for it is your life.

14 Do not set foot on the path of the wicked or walk in the way of evildoers.

15 Avoid it, do not travel on it; turn from it and go on your way.

16 For they cannot rest until they do evil; they are robbed of sleep till they make someone stumble.

17 They eat the bread of wickedness and drink the wine of violence.

18 The path of the righteous is like the morning sun, shining ever brighter till the full light of day.

19 But the way of the wicked is like deep darkness; they do not know what makes them stumble.

20 My son, pay attention to what I say; turn your ear to my words.

21 Do not let them out of your sight, keep them within your heart;

22 for they are life to those who find them and health to one's whole body.

23 Above all else, guard your heart, for everything you do flows from it.

24 Keep your mouth free of perversity; keep corrupt talk far from your lips.

25 Let your eyes look straight ahead; fix your gaze directly before you.

26 Give careful thought to the paths for your feet and be steadfast in all your ways.

27 Do not turn to the right or the left; keep your foot from evil.

Isaiah 2:2-3

2 In the last days the mountain of the Lord's temple will be established as the highest of the mountains; it will be exalted above the hills, and all nations will stream to it.

3 Many peoples will come and say, "Come, let us go up to the mountain of the Lord, to the temple of the God of Jacob. He will teach us his ways, so that we may walk in his paths."

About the Author

PETER THOMAS has served as director of YWAM Fortaleza (Youth with a Mission) since 2010 and has been in missions since 2000 in Brazil.

Before arriving in Brazil, Peter taught Mathematics at Bournemouth Grammar School for Boys for seven years after having graduated in Biochemical Engineering from Swansea University.

Peter is English, of Welsh descent, and married to Selma, his Brazilian wife of 19 years. They have two children, Danny (16) and Isabella (9), both born in Brazil.

Peter and Selma are dedicated to the discipleship of young people with Peter's passion in discipleship of teenage boys, and, as a family, their calling is to Family Ministries. Peter and Selma ran a restoration home for ex-Street Boys for 10 years.

Contact Information
psthomas2000@hotmail.com
Instagram: toclimbamountain
facebook: peter thomas
www.ywamfortaleza.org.br

Lightning Source UK Ltd.
Milton Keynes UK
UKHW022154170620
365168UK00011B/639